Music of the Inner Lakes

Music of the Inner Lakes

Stories by Roger Sheffer

Minnesota Voices Project Number 89
New Rivers Press 1999

First edition
Library of Congress Card Catalog Number: 98-89720
ISBN: 0-89823-193-0
Book design and typesetting by Percolator
Cover painting: *Door of Vain Regret,* by Tom Bartek, acrylic, 32 by 40 inches, 1988
Printed in Canada

"Bald Soprano" and "The Violin" were first published in *Laurel Review.*
"Music of the Inner Lakes" was published in *The Missouri Review.*

New Rivers Press is a nonprofit literary press dedicated to publishing
the very best emerging writers in our region, nation, and world.

The publication of *Music of the Inner Lakes* has been made possible by
generous grants from the Jerome Foundation; the North Dakota Council
on the Arts; and the Dayton Hudson Foundation on behalf of Dayton's,
Mervyn's California, and Target Stores.

This activity is made possible in part by a grant provided by the Minnesota
State Arts Board, through an appropriation by the Minnesota State Legislature.
In addition, this activity is supported in part by a grant from the National
Endowment for the Arts.

Additional support has been provided by the General Mills Foundation,
the McKnight Foundation, the Star Tribune Foundation, and the
contributing members of New Rivers Press.

New Rivers Press
420 North Fifth Street
Minneapolis, MN 55401

www.newriverspress.org

To the choirs of

Burnt Hills United Methodist Church (Burnt Hills, New York)
St. John's United Methodist Church (Sarasota, Florida)
St. John's Episcopal Church (Mankato, Minnesota)

Contents

Bald
Soprano

John moved through the empty church, feeling his way in the near dark, counting pews as he touched them gently. The echo of his high-heeled shoes startled him and he lunged forward, almost fell. He found a place to sit, twelve pews from where he had started counting. He took off his straw hat and rubbed the top of his head. Bald. And freezing. The cold from the top of his head pulsed down his neck, his spine, all the way to his rump. He put the hat back on and tried to relax enough so he could hear the choir, who were still up in the balcony, buzzing and chatting. Come on, he thought, get on with it. Make some goddamn music. He unsnapped the earring from his right ear and felt it for a moment. Gold? Silver? Plastic? The earring slipped from his arthritic fingers and rolled onto the floor. "Jesus," he muttered, then covered his mouth.

Behind and above him, the voices still chattered.

He cleared his throat and said, "What the hell's going on tonight?" He needed to hear an anthem come out of those voices, so he'd know how things stood. Or one verse of a hymn. Then he could leave. Nobody would have seen him in his hat and dress. On Halloween night, he had come to choir rehearsal disguised as a soprano, then lost his nerve halfway up the stairs.

"Somebody down there?" a voice called from the loft, and then a flashlight searched the sanctuary. "I heard coughing."

John looked around for the cougher. His weak eyes hadn't adjusted yet, and he had thought he was alone in the place.

"Hey, you down there," a baritone called out. "Turn off the lights when you leave."

"What lights?" John said softly. He looked over his shoulder and saw a faint glow from the vestibule, ten watts at most. The loft was dark. The stained glass lit up in flashes of orange and green when a car drove by on Route 30. John felt he was not alone. The other figure in the sanctuary did not come into focus, remaining a gray-brown shadow against the far wall. The cougher.

"Happy Halloween," John said, then waited for an answer. "Hope I didn't scare you."

The person did not move, did not speak.

John took off his hat. "It's just me, the bald soprano, ha-ha-ha!"

Instead of laughing, the person coughed. Coughed hard, hacking and wheezing.

"Tell me something," John said. "What part do you sing?"

Another cough.

"So, at least you're alive, whoever you are. I was starting to think you were only the shadow of a shade. Come on over here where I can see you better."

This man or woman stopped coughing but did not move.

"Come on over. I won't bite."

"Okay." The voice was rough, unmusical, barely audible. John assumed it was a man. No woman had a voice that low.

"Don't be a stranger."

"I don't wanna get too close," the man said, from across the aisle. "I got this bad cold or something. I just came in here to meditate for a moment and then I'll be on my way and you can have your privacy."

"I don't want my privacy. I have too much privacy for my own damn good!"

The man let John's remark echo before speaking again. "The choir sang for a while."

"They did? When did they start?"

"Jeez, I dunno. Don't have a watch. Maybe a couple hours ago. Then they talked. Then you came around. Clunk, clunk, clunk."

"Were they any good?"

"Who am I to judge?" the man said. "I never sung a right note in my entire life."

"How old are you?"

"What's that got to do with it?"

"I was just gonna say, it's never too late." John thought for a moment. "That choir might be looking for new people."

"What about you?"

"Heck, I'm too old. I'd like to sing the melody but they'd never let me sing with the sopranos. And my eyes are bad. I couldn't find the notes for the other parts."

"Find them? Where are they?"

"On the page somewhere. So I stick to the melodies these days, when they let me sing. And I'll tell you exactly how old I am. Seventy-five. Do I look it?"

"In this light I can't even tell whether you're bald or some long-haired hippy. I broke my only pair of glasses. I been driving down Route 30, feeling my way with the tires, you know how it is? Then I see this cross all lit up and I make a left turn and here I am sitting in a church. I don't even know what kind of church this is."

"Methodist. How old are you?"

"Too old."

"You sound forty. That's nothing, believe me. I've got two kids, one forty, one a little younger, but I forget how much. Helen used to keep track of those things. If they could see me now, they'd probably put me away. The bald soprano, singing in the looney bin. I don't know what the heck I'm doing here. Maybe you can tell me."

"You don't go around dressed that way all the time, do you?"

John laughed. "They'd pick me up and put me somewhere, wouldn't they?"

"They might."

"No, this get-up was just to give my old friends a laugh. They know me. I've done it before. They wouldn't put me away." He shivered slightly, believing for a second that they might. "It's a Halloween tradition. Every seven years Halloween falls on a choir rehearsal night. I once came dressed as a half note."

"Did they?"

"Did they what?"

"Did they laugh?"

"Today?"

"Yeah, today."

"No, I chickened out before I even made it to the top of the stairs. I don't think my friends come around here anymore, quite frankly. Maybe they're all dead. I don't know what's happened to the choir. None of my old friends up there, far as I can tell."

"They're gone. They sang and they're gone."

"It's all over then."

"But they'll be back next week, right? Don't choirs do that? Come back the next week and sing the same crap all over again?"

"I guess you don't like music."

The man said nothing.

"What's your name?"

The man hesitated. "Call me Howard."

"Any guy named Howard ought to be able to sing a few right notes."

"Afraid not."

"Oh come on, Howie."

"Howard."

"We don't have to look at the music or anything, if that's a problem for you. Music scares people sometimes—all those notes scattered on the page like a mess of beetles. That puts them off and they never wanna sing and they're satisfied to pay other people to make their music for them, which is a shame." He sat quietly for a moment and remembered the old days. "My boy was like that. John Jr. flunked music all the way through elementary school, can you believe it? You'd think he'd love it, with both his Mom and Dad in the choir and his big sister getting the lead part in her high school musical. My boy wouldn't have anything to do with the youth choir. Ran away from home when we even mentioned the possibility."

"Sounds like me."

"You ran away from home?"

"Many times."

"Because they made you sing?"

"It was worse than that, but I won't say how much."

John squinted toward the stranger, but Howard was still just an outline. "You and I could never read the music in this light, so it doesn't matter if one of us is illiterate."

"Illiterate?"

"No offense. I know most of that stuff by heart, the hymns, the amens, the responses. I learned the notes fast, got my face out of the music, and fixed my eyes on the choir director. You wouldn't believe some of those old ducks in the choir, they'd been singing these amens and responses, the same ones, the past thirty years and they still had to stare at the music all the time and make sure they got all the notes right! Ha! They were always a beat behind the conductor!"

Howard made no response.

"You never sang anything in your life?"

"Nope."

"Not even in school when they made you do it?"

"I moved my lips. They never bothered me about it, like you did to your John Jr." The man coughed a dozen times. "I can't barely talk. I must have pneumonia."

"What do you do?"

"Do?"

"Do you work?"

"You really wanna know?"

"I just thought, if you used your voice quite a bit on the job, maybe I could give you a few tips about taking good care of the old vocal cords. Like me—do I sound like I'm seventy-five?"

"I guess not."

"Of course I don't," John said, touching the loose folds of his neck. "When the voice doesn't age, the entire person seems a lot younger. You'd probably think I was fifty, or even younger, if I hadn't told you."

"Possibly."

"And believe it or not, I used my voice every minute of the working day, forty-five years of it. On the phone, face-to-face, I never stopped talking for a minute. I sold insurance. State Farm."

"Don't try and sell me no insurance, man."

"That's not what I'm all about, Howie. Besides, I'm retired ten years. I started to go deaf, and the boss made some hints about how I'd enjoy being retired. I don't enjoy it. I'm seventy-five and I should still be working every day."

Howard said nothing.

"The way you've been coughing, Howie, it's not good for the voice. You smoke?"

"Now and then."

"So did my Helen. Pack a day, which is moderate. Still sang beautiful, solid and deep, but she might have been a wonderful soprano
without the cigarettes. We needed sopranos back then, and she just
couldn't hit the notes. We were up to our necks in altos." He laughed,
thinking of what he had said. It sounded kind of dirty when he thought
of it—as if he were in a pond full of altos, and the altos were swim-
ming around like otters or dolphins.

"What are you getting at, mister?"

"I don't know. I'm an old man. My wife is dead. My kids are gone.
My choir is gone. Maybe I should have been paying attention at some
point. I'm sitting here in a dress on Halloween night and nobody's
laughing." He looked up at the dim vaulted ceiling and laughed,
although he could just as easily have cried. "Listen to the sound, the
way it echoes up there. Beautiful. You know, Howie, this church we're
sitting in right now has the best acoustics of any place in town. You
picked a good one. A person doesn't have to sing loud in here. You just
have to open your mouth and the song pretty much flies out on its
own. Listen." John let out a note somewhere around middle C, somewhere between AHHHH and EHHHH. He put a curl of vibrato on
the end, waited for Howard's reaction.

"Hey, you're not bad."

"I sang the solos, Howie. Forty years ago I did, when I was in my
prime, my mid-thirties."

"I'm older than that. It's too late, man. Too late for me already." A
passing headlight profiled Howard's face. John could see that he had
a beard.

"That beard real? Or part of a costume?"

"Real. Why would I wear a costume?"

"Halloween."

"It ain't Halloween, man. I don't know what day it is, but I know
for sure it ain't Halloween."

John touched his dress, felt how it only came down to his knees.
He was sure it had been mid-calf on Helen. The weather was too cold
to be wearing a summer dress. He wondered what month it was, but
decided not to ask. Howard needed help, and John didn't want the
guy to think he was dealing with a complete lunatic.

"Well, the whole thing was a practical joke," John finally said, touching a loose thread along the hem. "I'm famous for them."

"I never heard of you."

John took no offense. "What's the lowest note you can hit? Way, way down in the chest. That's where we'll start you out."

"Lowest note?"

"I'm not asking you to say what it is—A, B, C—I just want you to rumble down there and hit your lowest note."

Howard rumbled on the C two octaves below middle. John didn't hear him.

"Don't be shy about it, young fella. Pretend you're like a truck, like a jet plane."

"I did what you said."

"Then I guess you better go higher. I didn't realize I was deaf down there. Thought it was just the high notes I was missing. You learn something new every day. You learn about your limitations."

Howard did nothing.

"Make like a bee, Howie."

"I wish you'd quit calling me that. Howard is my name."

"Make like a bee, Howard."

"You gotta show me what you mean."

John imitated a bee, vibrating the sound in his nose as he hovered around the middle of his range. "I can do this when my throat is sore, like yours is. I can do this any day, any place, even when I have laryngitis. And it's good for me. I do it all day long. That's what keeps my voice sounding so young."

"They'd put you away. You in the dress, making a sound like a bee."

"You're right," John laughed. "Maybe when I'm driving alone in my car I could make strange sounds and nobody would notice. Or sitting here in church with just one other person who isn't going to make snap judgments about me." He hummed again. "It rattles the teeth. I still have my own teeth."

"More than I can say." Howard paused for a few seconds. "All this bee stuff. It don't sound much like music to me. Just a bunch of noise."

"Warm-ups, Howard. Choir singers do very strange things, just to loosen up the vocal cords. We yodel, we scream, we act like complete idiots. Just so we don't get tired fifteen minutes down the road and start scratching our throats when the choir director gets this notion that we should sound like angels."

"You warmed up, man?"

"Sure am."

"Well, then, sing something. I can tell you're just dying to sing for me."

"What's your pleasure?"

"You know country?"

"Country?"

"I guess you don't," Howard sighed.

" 'My Country, 'Tis of Thee.' I can do that, if that's country. No problem, bud." John proceeded to sing the first verse. He only needed six notes and he changed key only once.

"You have no idea how much I hate that song."

"I sang it that bad, huh?"

"No, you were okay. I meant the song. I hate it."

"It's a good song, Howard."

"I can't even judge. All I know is I hated it ever since I was a kid. Maybe some teacher made me sing a solo just to torture me like they always did. They'd waste the whole class period, making one kid sing through it all by himself, if it took that long. I remember sitting there and laughing."

"Then you pick it out. You pick out the song."

"Country. I know some folk. I used to listen to it. The way things are today I'm starting to remember something called 'Chilly Winds.' Boy, that's an old number. I don't suppose you know it. It's old, but not that old. It's by John Phillips."

John smiled, thinking of high school band. "The March King."

"What? The March King? I'm talking about a song by this guy that was the head of the Mamas and the Papas."

"Your father wrote a song?"

"No, man, listen to me! I'm not talking about my damn father."

"I have no idea what you are talking about, Howie, and I feel very sorry for you."

"I'm talking about a song, man, that's all."

"Then sing it for me."

"Yeah, sure."

"Just say the words, Howard. I'll put a tune on it."

Howard was silent.

"Howard? You still with me?"

"Tryin' to remember the words, you old fart."

"Don't talk like that in church."

Howard sang one verse of the song. John hoped he'd keep going, do another verse. Any music, even as rough as Howard's, gave him pleasure.

"I heard a few notes in there."

"Low notes, one or two." Howard cleared his throat, but didn't cough. "I guess you were right, John. The room makes it sound good. You weren't singing along, were you?"

"Hardly," he laughed. "I don't know the song! You're just teaching it to me for the first time."

They tried again—Howard on the bass, John an octave higher. The bald soprano. They sang the first verse several times, and then Howard began to remember the rest of it. He sang about leaving in the springtime, not coming back till fall. "If I can forget you, I might not come back at all." John didn't think about the words. He'd screw them up if he did—that was one of his weaknesses as a singer. But he liked the tune, the casual rhythm. Even when he'd forgotten everything else, he would hang on to a tune, and his head was full of them. But the way he was now, so forgetful, the tunes were useless. He'd pull them out on the wrong occasion and make a fool of himself. This one was simple, innocent. He could hum it in the car on the way home.

Car keys. He frisked himself. His dress had no pockets.

He stopped singing. "Say, Howie?"

No answer.

"Howie, now don't you go silent on me." John tried to focus on the edges of things, but there were no edges. "Howie, I'm gonna need some help from you now."

He heard a car backfire, out on the highway. The furnace kicked on, covering the sound of traffic.

"Howie?"

After a minute the furnace kicked off. John sat in the pew, shivering. The tune flew out of his head, forever, as if he'd never heard it, never met the guy. He got down on his knees and felt around on the floor until he touched something round and hard. He thought he'd found his other earring, but there was no clasp on it. He held the object to his nose. It smelled like chocolate. He set it down on the pew. Maybe later. When had he eaten? Where had he eaten? Where had he come from that day? He could not even remember getting dressed, whether he'd worn this outfit all day, or the day before and then slept all night in it, whether anybody had actually seen him dressed this way.

He felt around on the pew. He picked up an object that was round and hard. Where did that come from? Didn't I just ask that question? He touched the hem of his dress, picked at the loose thread, then pulled hard, until the thread snapped. He held the thread in both hands and fingered it from end to end, as if it would produce a sound—not music, but at least a voice that would tell him what to do next, or take him back and connect him with everything he had done.

Brigadoons

I've just started picking up *Brigadoon* on my car radio, rough fragments of an old chorus. The music could break into a thousand inaudible pieces if the car bounced the wrong way. My entire brain could fall apart. I turn off the air conditioner, keep the windows rolled up. As the road winds northwest out of the valley, the station keeps gargling and spitting. I can't tap it any clearer, and finally everything is lost in a diminishing buzz. So I play the melodies in my head, one or two songs half-remembered from my own performance, high school, not far from here and decades ago.

My sister lives in these mountains—in a permanent haze. Alice can't take care of herself much longer, only sixty-two, but you might guess seventy or eighty, to look at her—the way she disconnects from her environment, tunes out her company, and shakes into a blur, flickering like a woman in a silent movie, kind of backing away from the camera as if embarrassed to be seen by strangers so many years after her death. My theory is that my sister has grown old fast because her months are longer, the hard winter ones. Her town must be the opposite of Brigadoon, which disappears every hundred years, reappears for a day, goes to sleep again, hardly ages. In the anti-Brigadoon where Alice lives, January has fifty days, February, a hundred. During those added days of winter, my sister's hair turns gray and her teeth fall out.

Around 1980 she began to live exclusively in the past. When I called, she would immediately say to me, in her dried-out and deeply aggrieved voice, "Watch what you say or I'll hang up. You know the rules."

"Okay. How's your garden?"

"Gone to weeds," she coughed. "Stick to the past, or I *will* hang up. I don't think you really want to talk to me, just torture me."

"High school," I said.

"All right."

"Your time or mine?"

"Older is better."

So we would review her dazzling theatrical career, which ended with her graduation from high school. Alice was seven years ahead of me at Ballston Spa, and quite the actress—stunning as Katharina in *Taming of the Shrew*. Then she played Elizabeth in *Pride and Prejudice*. Completely convincing. She lived in that century for a month, spoke with a British accent, wore her costumes at home. When I entered high school, the teachers had not forgotten her and they asked about her career. Had she appeared in any movies? No. Surely, Alice had become a star. Nothing like that, I replied. She was working in an office supply company in Schenectady, had dropped out of college, married at twenty, and was now a widow. But that makes her sound so old! Children? None. What a shame; you tell her to stop by and talk with us! Schenectady isn't far from here.

In my heyday, the school staged a Broadway musical every spring, unabridged, with orchestra accompaniment. *Oklahoma, Carousel, Most Happy Fella*. I was a better singer than actor. They cast these shows by voice instead of body type, so I was given several good roles in high school. Baritone parts. Romantic leads. I was Tommy in *Brigadoon*. Many years later, my sister could describe my performance in such detail that you might have thought she had preserved it on videotape, but this was 1958, and the school didn't even have a reel-to-reel audio-tape recorder. Just a camera, for black-and-white photographs that have disappeared.

"You walked like an old man," Alice said.

"Oh God."

"Well, everyone was awkward. Fiona was pretty, but her voice couldn't stand up to yours. It was like the voice of a baby."

"No, it wasn't."

"You couldn't hear this because you were up there singing your own part, but I kept thinking, Shirley Temple, or Betty Boop. And you know who would have been perfect? Me! I could have sung the part of Fiona the way it was meant to be sung!" Her voice seemed younger for a moment, not so dead and dry, as if it had only been resting, dormant, inside a hard shell. "Except it might have looked bad—brother and sister singing a love duet, holding hands and gazing into each other's eyes."

"People would have laughed. They were laughing at me anyway, I always thought."

"There were comic elements, especially Meg, who, by the way, really did attend her own mother's wedding. The show seemed miscast. Jeannie had a better voice than Fiona, but of course she was in love with Charlie. I mean, she really was. I'm sure you knew."

"Alice," I would say, "none of those affairs matter now."

"Oh, but they do. They're the only thing that matters."

"Nothing left of it. We're living in a different world now."

"Speak for yourself."

I could be talking with my grandmother, there's such an age gap between us.

The static clears, and the ancient violins cut through time and space. The Fiona who sings on my car radio is sweet, approachable, permanently eighteen. She reminds me of Shirley Jones, but less famous, a decade older, possibly Barbara Cook or Pamela Britton.

"Didn't you know, Tommy, that you're all I'm thinking of—"

Lord, I say to myself, stepping on the brakes from the shock of the idea. Did Fiona sing those words to me? To me? The girl who played Fiona had to believe in what she was singing, if only for a brief moment. Having forgotten her real name, I always think of her as Fiona.

"And how can you go, Tommy—"

A beautiful girl was sad to see me go? Hard to fix such a fact in my mind, that a stage kiss was more than skin deep. Back in April 1958, dealing with the part of Tommy, I concentrated on my notes, the words—as written—and if the feeling came out, hey, terrific, but I wasn't going to press it. Words and notes occupied my entire being.

I was a robot, pretending to be human, my head almost detached from my body. "You and the world we knew will . . ." The verb escapes me. But I pick up the lyrics a few measures later: "You're part of me from this day on!"

I once said to Alice, "Every trace of *Brigadoon* is gone. It isn't even a memory of a memory. It doesn't move me."

"How can you say such a thing? It'll creep up on you, and then capture you, hold you tight. So tight it'll scare you."

"Nope."

"Remember that wonderful John Sampson who played Petruchio when I was Katharina? He was just gorgeous."

"He in the movies?"

"Died a long time ago, strangled himself while lifting weights. He was gorgeous. I can see him right now. In his tights, his curly blond hair, his sweet face. He spanked me."

"In the play, yeah, I remember."

"Not just in the play, dear brother. In real life. Whatever happened to your Fiona?"

"Slipped into a wrinkle in time. Never grew old." Fiona skipped college, got married right after high school, had a couple of babies. This is what must have happened. She must have had a terrible life in real time and space. A trailer court and a beer belly, toothless.

"And you're looking for that wrinkle."

"No, I was miserable every night. Couldn't wait until the show was over. I was sure I'd screw up something. I was always walking the wrong way, forgetting lines."

"You'd go back," she said. "If you could find it."

"What—and be stuck in that sappy musical, condemned to sing my part over and over? Or perhaps the sequel."

"The sequel?"

"Like, how everybody got along after the curtain."

"The cast party?"

"No, I mean, the things that happened to Tommy and Fiona and Charlie and Bonnie Jean."

"You're not serious," she said.

"I think they led boring lives in paradise. They just kept singing that damn chorus over and over. That was the sequel."

I don't particularly care for the baritone on my car radio, the original-cast Tommy. Alfred Drake is probably not the name on his birth
certificate. Why is it okay for Broadway stars to sing sharp? His vibrato
works funny—the lower edge hits the note, the higher edge flutters a
quarter tone too high. Vibrato should work the other way. This guy
must have been a terrific actor. He must have looked great on stage.

I sang better.

The signal is strong. Tommy and Fiona are singing "The Heather
on the Hill." I come to the place on my route where I hang a right if
the traffic signal is red, go straight if it's green. The two roads come
together again three miles later. The road to the right winds through
an old village which is in the process of becoming a hamlet, or whatever term they have for such a regression. I heard on the news that
this place wants its village status legally revoked, so as to save money
on various kinds of services mandated by the legislature. Politically, it
will disappear. I'm driving through at thirty-five. It's a one-street deal
that follows a winding stream up into the foothills, a loose chain of
general store and post office and body shop and forty white houses.
They have sidewalks. When they're no longer a village, somebody will
no doubt roll up the sidewalks and take them away.

With *Brigadoon,* all you had to do was hold your breath, and the
village disappeared. Tommy, the American visitor who, with his cyn-
ical friend (I forget his name—a nonsinging part), stumbled upon
Brigadoon while on vacation, was told if he stayed, well, here's the
dilemma—he'd be making a one-hundred-year commitment. Nope,
can't do it, not even for love. But now Tommy is back in Scotland, and
for some reason the people of Brigadoon have not quite resealed the
envelope, they have bent time and space to accommodate him, and
the music starts tumbling into our world, Tommy is drawn back into
the arms of Fiona. If he ever gets out again, it will be a hundred years
later or some multiple of a hundred, and I hardly think the world will
be a better place.

An entire muscle of remorse flexes down the middle of my face
as I consider how bad the world will be in a hundred years. Tommy's
friend's name was Jeff. He died in a motorcycle accident, not in the
show, but in real life. In my yearbook, which I have misplaced, he
wrote something ironic, about how I was the lucky one, the one who

had been taken back into Paradise. He signed his name that way—
"Jeff," in quotes.

There are several Brigadoons:
1. The Brigadoon of Lerner and Loewe's imagination. Or the Brigadoon of folklore, where they might have found the idea for the musical, if they didn't make up the story from scratch.
2. The Brigadoon of Broadway, and this original-cast album. Alfred Drake and the others, singers whose voices have broken. Dancers now bedridden and incontinent.
3. The movie (Gene Kelly and Cyd Charisse, dancing and singing against impossible pastel skies).
4. My high school. It wasn't quite the same. We screwed up more than a few lines, left out whole pages. Our set was different. It didn't look Scottish, more like Bavarian, recycled from *The Student Prince.* Damn, where is that set? We struck the set, but we didn't burn the pieces. It exists somewhere. It's been re-painted. It was sealed up behind a wall. They're putting on the show again. Every twenty years. Every twenty years they unfold that set and some cast member comes tumbling out, rubs the dust from his or her eyes, and asks what scene we're in now.
5. The Brigadoon of memory and dreams, which my sister maintains for me.
6. The Brigadoon of now; the real Brigadoon, the village that will come to life after its one-hundred-year sleep, in Scotland. In fifty or sixty years? I'll be dead by then, damn it.

The morning after we struck our set, I slept late, exhausted from the performance, and even more, from trying to be amusing at the cast party. Although the star of the show, I was a flat character in real life, stuck to the wallpaper all night. My mother knocked on my bedroom door and said, "Don't you know what time it is?"

"What? Did I miss the bus?"

"It's Sunday. You missed church, but that's unimportant."

"Then let me sleep," I said. "I'll sleep right through to Monday. I'll sleep a whole year, a century."

"Someone's on the phone for you."

"For me? Nobody ever calls me."

"She asked for Tommy, which I figured out right away."

"Who is it?"

"She didn't say."

"Could you take a message for me? I can barely talk. I must be coming down with laryngitis."

"All right." Then she said, "You and your sister."

"What?"

"You take it much too seriously."

I awoke again, and lingered at the table sipping my orange juice. My sister, home for a long visit, came into the room. She sat down across from me and handed me a note, but held on to it for a moment.

"Isn't this interesting?" she said.

"Must be that phone call when I was sleeping."

"Fiona," she said with a smile. "You don't know a Fiona."

"*Brigadoon*," I said. "Some of the cast can't tell the difference between real life and make-believe. They've been going around school calling each other by their characters' names. I hope they'll stop, now that the damn show is over. It's silly."

"We always did that."

"I didn't."

"John and I. Petruchio and I." Alice tapped her knife on the table. "Well, what did your girlfriend say?"

I handed back to her the note that my mother had taken. Alice read it aloud, faking a Scottish accent—"Come back, Tommy. Come back, there's still a chance for you," and she proceeded to sing Fiona's solos while I covered my ears in embarrassment.

When the fog dissolves along this mountain road, this valley through which I've driven a hundred times on the way to my sister's house, I'm always disappointed. I deserve more than the usual A-frame chalets, for sale the past ten years, the dead gas stations, former bait shops, tourist information centers crumbling in the damp.

How about a sword dance?

Or a sweet female arm beckoning, as the chorus swells?

Now I climb another hill, layering up into the highest range, the town where she lives. The wiper will not clear the rain, but I've driven this road by feel, and the more the road falls apart, the more it conforms to my memory, my instinct of how to get there.

Driving along a newly constructed road in an upstate county, you will often see signs that have been covered with brown trash bags. And you wonder what message is being concealed, what new speed limit, what information not yet relevant. Other signs have been painted over—not by vandals, but by highway officials, as if the town has been renamed, or there's some other destination, still real, if one turns right, while the old one has become unreal, a blank space on the map. To leave its name on the green sign would be to raise unrealistic expectations on the part of strangers, those who visit a place not because they have any business there, but because they like its name and believe they could become permanently lost there.

The last chorus of *Brigadoon* breaks into static. Too many mountains in the way. Sometimes you get Vermont Public Radio up here, if the valleys line up properly. Way over at the other end, around 107.5, you get religion, or country. I'll take the static, the swish of my tires.

My sister's town isn't much of a town, really. A church, a store (post office, summers only), a phone company switching station in a concrete box, a big pyramid of dirt next to the town garage, a dark log tavern, several trailers that have been added onto and roofed over, various old dogs who think they own the place, a collapsed barn, and the like. She lives there because, long ago, she inherited this property from her late husband's family. They were the "first family" of this town.

Now everything is gone. Carted away. Replaced by trees. The mists recede and I can make out the familiar three-pointed mountain as I cross the stream on the five-ton-limit bridge (warning sign removed, but otherwise the same). I'm cresting where my sister's house should be, and of course it isn't there. The myth of her town must be that it exists in this world one hundred years, goes away for a single day, then comes back for another hundred, the exact reverse of Brigadoon. And I happened to pick the day of nonexistence. There could be many towns in this world that fade out for a day every hundred years, where it wouldn't really matter, because they were so far off the beaten track that nobody would miss them if they were only gone that long.

My Last Piano

"**A**nd when did it arrive?" she asked, attaching her question to what he had just said. He hated it when she did that—too much like a duet. So he took a couple of long breaths before speaking again.

"About two weeks ago." He lifted the flimsy package from the night-stand and showed it to her. "It's a goddamn shirt."

"And how do you know that?"

"Because it's always an oxford button-down shirt. White or blue." He pressed the dark green wrapping paper, smudged it with his damp fingers, then examined his fingertips in the early-morning light that came through the window. "My mother thinks my size is medium. Fifteen-and-a-half collar. Thirty-four sleeve."

She grabbed the package from him and shook it. "Kind of heavy for an oxford shirt. What will you do with it?"

"Give it away," he said, taking it back with a firm yank.

"Why don't you send her your correct size?"

"She'd worry. She'd wonder what I was doing with an eighteen-inch neck." He returned the package to the nightstand, where it could stay for a year.

"Open it," she said. "Get dressed. Put it on."

"It won't fit."

"The shirt might fit me." She tore off the wrapping paper. He'd have to stop seeing this woman, who was much too eager to get into his things.

The day before his birthday one year, he stayed up past midnight. He had been born at two in the morning, which made it okay to open the gift from his parents—his only gift—at exactly that time. He slid the shirt out of its plastic wrapper, pulled the pins, the cardboard backing, inhaled the sweet vanilla that new shirts always smell like. And the next evening, when they finally called, his mother singing on the kitchen extension, his father breathing heavily on the bedroom phone and muttering in some feeble approximation of the happy birthday song, he confessed that he had celebrated early, opened the gift at two in the morning. The shirt had fit perfectly and he had worn it to work.

Of course, that birthday present was in the ragbag now. He had wiped up grease with it.

"It's not a shirt!" She held up the shirt-size plastic bag and sighed in disappointment. "Not even close."

"Music! Goddamn, what is my mother sending me that stuff for?"

"You don't even play. It's piano music, right?"

"Piano and voice." He took it from her and held it out of sight, over the edge on his side of the bed. "I used to play."

"You did? Why didn't you tell me?"

"Because I was terrible."

"And so, you're saying, you didn't want me to hear you play because, you claim, you were terrible?" She scratched her head. Her hair was too short and too red, almost purple. "I don't believe that for a minute."

"It's true."

"You've been hiding something from me."

"No, I haven't. Music isn't part of my life. I gave up on music several years ago. So I'm hiding nothing."

She stood up from the bed and walked out of the room, naked. Her left elbow knocked against the doorframe. She walked on her heels, in a syncopated rhythm, as if her bones didn't quite fit together. The off-beat footsteps came to a stop in the living room, on the floorboard that vibrated above a metal heat duct—twango, twango. "Hey!" she yelled. "You could have a piano right here. I found the perfect place for it."

He remained seated on the bed and spoke in a normal voice. "Pianos always go out of tune. Like, you bring in some guy and he spends a couple hours tuning the damn thing, and as soon as he's out the door, you play two notes together—an F and an A in the next octave. It sounds like crap."

"Come out here, I wanna show you something."

"I'm staying where I am."

"It's an outline of a piano in the wallpaper. The green is less faded there, the pink in the flowers. And I can see exactly where the piano stood, the indentations in the floor, perfectly spaced."

"Probably a dresser. A stereo cabinet."

"A piano."

"Not while I've lived here."

"And so, you're telling me, you never had a piano."

"Not here."

"In the past, then."

He flexed his fingers as he lay back in bed. What the heck. He told her about the piano.

He had bought a used mahogany Wurlitzer spinet from the music store on Central Avenue. This was in Albany, years ago. The movers carried it up the curved stairs to his old second-floor apartment, yelling curses that vibrated on the lower strings. One of the guys hurt his finger angling the piano through the door and smeared blood on the white plaster. There were no bandages in the medicine cabinet, so they wrapped the finger in a handkerchief.

That week his girlfriend Linda came over with her *Best of Broadway* book. He screwed up the accompaniment, even though it was simplified. He felt some kind of sympathetic pain in one finger. They switched places. He stood up and sang, and there was a line in a song from *Brigadoon* where you were supposed to pick a pronoun according to your gender. The obvious choice was to sing "her," but he slipped up and sang "him." Linda stopped playing, crashing on a minor chord.

"What?" She looked at him.

"Innocent mistake."

"Really?" She squinted at the music.

"What are you saying?"

"I'm saying there's no such thing as an innocent mistake."

They did a couple more songs out of the book but she never visited his apartment again.

"And what happened to the Wurlitzer?"

"It dissolved. It no longer exists."

"Come on." They were still in separate rooms. She was talking loud; he was speaking just above a whisper, and yet she heard him. This was another thing about her that he did not like.

"All right. When I moved, I sold it to my best friend Gary. He was staying in town to finish his last year of grad school. I sold it to him for a hundred bucks. Cost me almost a thousand."

"That was your last piano?"

"Yeah, my last piano. Good title for a song."

"And you write music, too?"

"I didn't say that."

My last piano. The song would work in three-four time, not too fast, something like, *We lived ten years above the music store. The notes they played came up through the floor, and you told me all the songs you used to know.* And so on, how the people in that apartment would make up words to go with the music they heard. The song would almost write itself, in his head, even while he talked, using words that might work their way into it. "Gary called me up not too long ago. July. He still has the piano. His kids are learning to play on that piano."

"Could have been your kids. Did you ever think about that?"

"My Wurlitzer has never gone out of tune," he said. "Gary never had to bring in the tuner. I hardly believe that. Every piano goes out of tune, eventually, what with the heat, humidity, lack of humidity, kids walking all over the keys." Tiny children. That's what he imagined, tiny children jumping from key to key, falling, then pulling themselves up with their sticky fingers.

"I can't ever tell when something is out of tune. People say, 'That's out of tune,' and it's a mystery to me. I can't tell the difference."

"You hear pretty well." Something to rhyme with "oh."

"But I don't know what the notes are. To me, they're all the same."

He put on his jeans and went into the living room, holding the plastic bag of music between thumb and index finger, ready to drop it into the nearest wastebasket. *And a few we made up, it was all so long ago.* Too many syllables.

She was touching the wall, tracing the line that marked where the top of the piano had been. "Put your next piano here," she said, indicating the shape of a piano the way a mime would.

"Get dressed." Next piano. That wouldn't make a very good song.

"This apartment is too empty."

"Did you see a birthday card anywhere? Did my mother include a card with the present?"

"No."

"My crazy mother must be cleaning out the house, down to the bare walls. You know, I gave her this music. I didn't say, 'Just hold it for me.' I said, 'It's yours, Mom. I'm through with music.' "

"Your mother knows you better than you know yourself. She's trying to help bring back that wonderful part of your life."

"She's losing her mind."

"She knows exactly what is missing from your life."

"I was no good."

"Let's go shopping for used pianos. Or new pianos."

"No."

"I'll get a ruler and measure the place where the old piano was. We can buy one that will fit exactly."

"Get dressed."

The same guys had removed the piano, and he had tipped them the second time, knowing that Gary wouldn't. Ten dollars each. He had touched their fingers while handing them the money.

Before they took the piano bench, he had removed the sheet music—mostly songs from the forties, the cheap paper starting to decompose, cracking along the edges. He liked these old arrangements, the piano parts much more subtle and interesting than the reductions one might find in anthologies. On the back, more songs were advertised, usually from the same movie, and they'd give you about four bars, then break it off where you really wanted to see the music keep going, in the middle of a word sometimes. "I'm putting all my eggs in one basket, I'm betting ev—"

A few days after getting rid of the piano, he took the music to his mother.

"What am I supposed to do with these?" she had asked, handing them back.

"Aren't they your favorites?"

"They don't bring back happy memories," she said quietly. His father was in the back yard, riding the Toro. When the mower got close to the house, they couldn't hear what they were saying to each other.

"But keep them for me, anyway," he said. "Please? I can't take all my junk with me to Ohio."

"Rita Hayworth is pretty old now," his mother had said, leaning back, squinting. "She sure doesn't look anything like that now." And then she took the music from him, pinched it in the middle. "Dick Haymes. So tragic. I think he's dead. He looks about twenty in this picture."

"They all smoked too much," he said.

"Rita Hayworth," his girlfriend said. She had put on her robe, loosely tied. It could come off again in a second.

"The one and only. She never sang anything."

"That poor woman is dead now." She touched the name through the plastic. "Top billing, higher than Gene Kelly. Must have been the pinnacle of her career. Who else is in this bag?" She slid the music out of the plastic. "Bing Crosby, Deanna Durbin, Dick Haymes—who the hell is he? Ethel Merman, Perry Como, Shirley Temple. Can I have that one?"

"You can have them all."

"But they're your birthday present. From your mother."

"She doesn't even know it's my birthday. Where's the card?"

His friend laid out the sheet music, fanlike, on the dining room table. "No card," she said. "But what is this little item? A program for a concert? It's very fancy. April 10th, 1976." She opened the program and a newspaper clipping fell on the rug. "Hey, look at that. Your name is in the headline. I'm discovering all kinds of things today."

"Shit."

"You did fine." She patted him on the shoulder. "It says you were 'a most accomplished accompanist.' "

"Say that twenty times real fast."

"I'd like to."

"I'd rather you didn't."

All right, so now he had the verse. And the chorus would go, *My last piano, they took it away last week. They hauled it down the stairs, while a tear ran down my cheek.* Terrible rhyme. Or maybe, *while I was taking a leak.* As if the piano had been stolen from him when he was vulnerable, attending to his human needs.

She sat on the couch and stared at the wall, the outline of what she thought was a piano. "Turns out I was right about you all along. You're a real musician."

"I've lost the touch."

"This afternoon we'll drive to the mall and look for a piano. A used piano. Heck, I'll buy you a cheap one. A birthday present! We could get it tuned."

"What for? Who the hell needs an accompanist?"

She rubbed her throat, hummed a couple of notes. "I do."

"But you don't sing."

She opened the Rita Hayworth music. "Everybody sings. Even Rita."

"That's not true, but go ahead—sing something."

She sang the first few words, "Long ago and far away," to no recognizable tune, very much like the beauty contestant on *Seinfeld*, Miss Rhode Island, who had been forced to change her talent genre at the last minute when Jerry dumped water on her trained pigeons.

"What do you think?" She laid the music on the end table, gave him a look.

He did not react. He was supposed to hug her or something, but held his hands behind his back, felt his fingers trembling, as if they knew the music to the song he had just written and only wanted a keyboard to let it out.

"I'd do much better with a piano," she said.

"There will be no piano."

"You keep saying that, but what if this happened? What if a piano just magically appeared—right here in this room, in the middle of the night?"

"I would have it removed."

Even in 1976, the songs had been old. The members of his studio had performed them in a long, narrow room at the City Museum on Washington Avenue, fifty in the audience. He accompanied for everybody—a dozen women, three men, all singing Gershwin and Porter and Kern.

Some of the singers were wonderful. Their voices floated. It was easy to play the piano under those floating voices, as if they had somehow cleared the way for him, taken out the interference that usually got in the way of making good music. Two or three of the women had been perfect, and he had loved them—at least while they sang. Two or three of the women had been very hard to love when they weren't singing.

But this woman, in his house right now—she could not sing. She might ask him to teach her, ask him to play the piano while she exercised her awful voice. Maybe she was faking how bad she was, the way he had sometimes done with his piano playing, held up his fingers in some fake gnarled pose and told people that he could no longer perform.

He walked back into the bedroom and lay on the bed, thinking, What shirt will I wear today? Good song title, good first line. *Does it even matter—when there isn't any music in my life? And what is even sadder, not that I'm much fatter—*

"Listen to me!" She kept talking at him from the other room, trying out the songs from the old music he had once played as an accompanist for professional singers. No recognizable tunes came from her mouth. Then she began to sing them all on "Ninety-nine Bottles of Beer on the Wall," as if, out of that atonal chaos, a rudimentary order had emerged. She had four notes, a tight little range centering around middle C, and she changed the key whenever the tune threatened to move beyond that range. Then she stopped.

"Forget the live music," he said. "We could put a stereo in that space."

"That won't even begin to do it," she said.

"Do what?"

"Fill the enormous gap in your existence."

She kept talking, but the only words in his mind were the lyrics to a song that seemed to have taken on a life of its own:

> *It might even make you sick. It isn't idle chatter.*
> *She wants to be my wife,*
> *I'll get a little organ, with colored keys and chick-a-boom,*
> *And play while she belts out a song*
> *That hits the walls and breaks the ears and clears the room*
> *When she admits that I was right and she was wrong.*

The Dead
Tenor

The boy came running out of the church wearing a black T-shirt that had a skeleton printed on it, back and front, like an X ray.

"That's terrible," Kathy said, stepping to the side to avoid being knocked over. "He wore that during the memorial service?"

"I don't think he did," John said. "I mean, he had on a robe over it. He was the acolyte."

"It was a nice service, for a nice man. Only twenty people showed up."

"Mostly the choir," John said.

"We were his 'family.' If he had a real family, he never told me about it."

"Me neither."

"And now it's just the two of you." Kathy lit a cigarette and inhaled deeply, closed her eyes, then opened them suddenly, as if some terrible thought had startled her. "We're down to two tenors."

"Yup," John said, folding the service leaflet and sticking it in his suitcoat pocket. "Just old Walter and me."

"Of course, if I keep smoking at this rate, I might end up in the tenor section."

"Not good for the voice."

"To switch from alto to tenor?"

"No, to keep smoking."

"Don't quote me," she said, glancing over her shoulder, "but I never guessed it would be Tom."

"Guessed?"

"That he would die first." She grabbed his elbow. "I mean, look at old Walter."

Ten yards down the sidewalk, Walter had dropped his service leaflet and was bent over trying to scrape it up with his fingers. After several feeble swipes, he just left it there and walked on unsteadily.

"Poor guy," John said.

"Walter has been on the edge of death ten years at least."

"He never misses church."

"But he's so fragile. I'm always afraid for him," she said, "that one day he'll just tip over and break. I'm always kind of reaching over to catch him, just in case." Walter did seem breakable. Thin wrists, neck, ankles.

"We'd be down to one tenor." Kathy pointed at John with her cigarette, then dropped it on the ground and stepped on it. She gave him a hard look, as if he were responsible for everything, even the cigarette she had dropped. "Of course, if Walter died, it wouldn't be so bad. The church is supposed to inherit his money. Close to a million dollars, all of it earmarked for the choir."

"How about Tom?"

"Oh, he didn't leave a cent," she said.

"Tom formed a barrier between us, kind of. Between Walter and me." John shaped an invisible barrier with his hands, about the width of a body. "I never really paid much attention to Walter. I'm just starting to notice him." John and Kathy watched him get into his car, the eternity it took to close the door. The boy in the skeleton T-shirt was kicking a stone across the parking lot.

"I never believed Tom would die like that," Kathy said.

"You know how he died?"

"No, I mean I just assumed he would go on singing forever. What was he? Sixty?"

"I don't know."

"I'm pretty sure he was two years older than Walter, and Walter is always telling me he hasn't hit sixty yet."

"He hasn't?" John shook his head. Walter looked at least sixty-five. Seventy. Much older than Tom.

"Maybe he never will."

Tom's empty seat took on a practical use. During church service Walter kept his hymnal and prayer book there. John liked having that space between them—he didn't want to catch some fatal disease from Walter. He kept wondering what had killed Tom, who had seemed so solid and real just two months ago, and had disappeared and then died without apparent cause. Walter kept fussing with his things on the chair.

"Makes a good desk for you," John said.

"Better than the floor." Walter coughed without covering his mouth. John held his breath. He could see droplets hanging in the bright shaft of sunlight. Walter wiped his mouth with the sleeve of his robe. "Don't you think?"

"Uh-huh."

"We ought to have actual desks, each with its own lamp, like the choristers at King's. I always step on my reading glasses. I've gone through a dozen pairs that way."

On Tom's old seat, Walter had stacked his books to make room for his dark leather glasses case, a box of Luden's cough drops, Maalox bottle, and Vicks inhaler. "Got a first-aid kit, too?" John whispered. "Iodine? Band-Aids?"

"Whatever for?"

"Your hands."

Walter's hands were badly scratched. He seemed surprised by the sight of them. "Oh, that's nothing."

"Who'd you get in a fight with?"

"Just my cat," he said, then dropped his hymnal. Walter could never hold his music steady. It was always exploding, flying into the air, gliding and drifting to distant places. Now that Tom no longer sat between them, John noticed many strange things about Walter. His socks didn't match. He crossed himself all the time. He practically sucked the chalice dry at Communion. He cleaned his glasses with a little spray bottle and dishcloth during the sermon. One time he dropped the spray bottle on the floor, and it rolled across the linoleum almost to the Communion rail. He sighed and got up from his kneeler, grabbing the hem of his cassock. When he passed the cross he genuflected, then bent over and retrieved his bottle, held it up for all to view. "It's just normal tap water," he said to the congregation, who were praying silently after the sermon. "Not holy water."

"You may be seated," the priest said.

"I promise. It won't happen again."

"Take it easy, Walter."

"I'm sorry."

After a month, the dead tenor was finally replaced—by a bass. So the men all shifted to the left, and the space between Walter and John was gone. Now Walter had to store his supplies under his chair and kneeler. He was always bumping into John, poking him with things as he retrieved them from the floor. One time he even reached over and grabbed John's left arm when he couldn't get up from his kneeler.

"What?" John said.

"I'm just a bit dizzy," Walter said. "I didn't mean anything by it. You think I'd attack you in church?"

"Attack me?"

"I wouldn't attack you." He paused and smiled. "I know you're happily married."

"You startled me," John said. "That's all."

"Were you asleep?"

"No," John said. "I wasn't asleep."

"You always have your eyes closed when I look at you. I'm looking at you right now, and your eyes are closed."

"Resting them."

"You're not very old," Walter said. "I bet you're not even forty."

"I'm over forty. How old are you?" John kept his eyes closed.

"You don't wanna know. But I can tell you I've been sitting in this same chair for thirty years."

"Uh-huh."

"I could feel my way around this damn place if I had to."

"Uh-huh."

"I could hang on to a younger person when we walked down the aisle. It would be perfectly innocent. You have good vision, don't you?"

As the post-Communion prayer ended, John opened his eyes and looked at the hymnal board. "Hymn number 453."

"What?"

"Get ready," John said sharply. "We're marching out on hymn number 453."

"You don't have to remind me about the order of worship."

"We're leaving now."

"All right, all right." Walter bent down to pick up his things, but couldn't straighten up. His back had gone out. They had to call an ambulance and carry him out of the church in a stretcher. As they brought him down the aisle, Walter kept shouting, "I'm sorry! I'm sorry!" although most of the congregation had gone home by then. The boy in the skeleton T-shirt stood at the door and watched.

Easter morning, the choir had lined up in the narthex, ready to march in pairs to the front of the church. John stood in formation without a marching partner.

"This happens all the time," a bass said. Norbert. It was the first Sunday of daylight savings, and a certain tenor had evidently failed to set his clock ahead. "Old Walter will prance in during the sermon, knock over a few candles on his way. Lots of noise. He likes the attention."

"Maybe his back went out again," John said.

"No, I just saw him," Kathy said. "His back is fine. He ducked into the closet to get his robe."

"Into," Norbert said, "and then out of. Except he's not really out of the closet, is he? Know what I mean?"

Kathy didn't get it right away, but a couple other basses laughed, rolled their eyes.

"We shouldn't joke about him," Kathy finally said. "We have no right to judge."

They were halfway to the altar before Walter slipped into place next to John. He placed his hand on one side of John's hymnal and began to sing off-key. The hymnal started shaking and John grabbed it away.

When they sat down after the Gloria, Walter said, "You'd treat me better if you knew me better."

John said nothing.

"This is the second worst morning of my entire life."

"Oh yeah?"

Walter inserted a honey lemon cough drop into his mouth, then made a loud sucking noise. "My cat died."

"I'm sorry."

"I'm shaking all over."

"Relax," John said. "You don't have to sing."

"Not sing? Are you kidding? You'd be all alone on the tenor part. I have to sing."

"No, I'll be okay," John said. "Just relax. Sit there. Don't kneel. Don't stand up."

"I can't believe it."

"Sorry about the cat."

"It's not the cat. It's the fact that I'm late. I'm never late. You know that."

"Right."

"I had an unbroken record. Thirty years, I was never late."

"You're here."

"Help me out this morning, please?" Walter said, touching John's left shoulder. "I forgot to pick up a program on the way in. You've gotta hold your program so I can see the words to the psalm. I have a one-inch range where I focus, then everything blurs."

"How's that?"

"Okay. Now tip it towards me ten degrees. Perfect."

They sang the psalm. Walter screwed up only two or three words. When they got to the litany, he messed up several times by saying the lector's lines, each time apologizing out loud, "I'm sorry," further confusing the matter.

They came to the part where the lector said, "For the special needs and concerns of this congregation." John called out, "For Walter and his cat."

And the lector said, "Hear us, O God."

At the Peace, Walter used both hands for his handshake. John felt nothing but bones, dry twigs, easily breakable. He pressed gently and said, "Just take it easy, buddy." And Walter said, "It gets harder and harder."

That Sunday, Walter went to the rail for the birthday blessing. The boy in the skeleton T-shirt stood next to him—his birthday, too. The priest asked the boy how old he was, and he said, "Twelve," in a voice much too deep for his angelic face. He dropped some coins into a special offering plate. Everybody said a prayer for him. And then the priest turned to Walter and smiled. "Here's a young man who must be getting close to thirty years old." The congregation laughed.

Walter stood up and faced them, head trembling. "Actually, if you start counting from when I joined the choir, then you're right. Close to thirty." And then, as he dropped an envelope into the plate—stuffed, perhaps, with hundred-dollar bills—the congregation said in unison, "O God, our times are in your hands: Look with favor, we pray, on your servant Walter, as he begins another year. Grant that he may grow in wisdom and grace, and strengthen his trust in your goodness all the days of his life, through Jesus Christ our Lord. Amen."

Back in his choir stall, Walter turned to John. "My birthday was two days ago."

"Oh?"

"Nobody remembered. Not a single card or phone call."

"Not even Kathy?"

"What? You think she's a close friend or something?"

"Isn't she?"

"She's just after my money," Walter said.

"I don't think so."

"All she wants to talk about is money. I have no close friends now." He waved toward the other people in the church. "If I didn't go up for my birthday blessing, who would even know I existed?"

"I'll mark it down for next year."

"Don't bother," Walter said. "Probably won't even happen."

"How old are you?"

"Never mind."

They had coffee and doughnuts afterward in the church social hall.

"My birthday party," Walter said softly. "At least I can pretend that's what this thing is. They've got a spice cake, no candles."

"I hate birthdays," John said, pouring himself another cup, noticing a slight tremor in his own hands. "I wish people wouldn't give me surprise parties, that kind of thing."

"Are you trying to make me think you envy me?"

"No," John said. "I'm just complaining."

"You shouldn't complain."

"I know."

"At least in your case, somebody makes a fuss," Walter said, gesturing with half a sugar doughnut. A burst of sugar landed on the sleeve of John's blazer. "And that counts for something in this life."

"I wouldn't mind if they'd just forget."

"Why?"

"I hate being reminded how close to fifty I am."

"You're not close to fifty."

"Yup," John said, rubbing the sugar dust from his sleeve. "Pretty darn close."

"I'm sure this will come as no surprise to you, but I'll never see fifty again." Walter looked at the clock on the wall. "Well, whaddya know. I'm an hour younger than I thought I was. Is time going backwards?"

"The clock is wrong."

"Is it really?"

"Yeah," John said. "They forgot to set it ahead."

"Sometimes I think I should have stayed in my mother a while longer. I was premature, you know."

"Oh."

"I arrived two months early." He sipped his coffee, scowled as if the coffee were hot, or bitter. Then he said, "I often use my prematurity as a fudge factor, when I feel too old. I tell myself that I'm actually two months younger than I am, which keeps me comfortably confused." He sat down on a folding chair.

"Sounds reasonable."

"My back almost went out again. Just now, standing and talking with you."

"Gotta be careful."

Walter swallowed the last of his doughnut. "Let's talk about Tom. Remember Tom?"

"Sure."

"It was his birthday this past week, too. He would have been up there with me."

John hesitated before he spoke. "Is there a birthday blessing for the dead?"

"Come here." Walter stood up and motioned for John to follow him into the kitchen. "Or maybe we should find another place to talk." He nodded toward Kathy and two other women who were wiping down the kitchen counters. "Come to my apartment."

"We're having dinner pretty soon."

"That's right. I forgot you were married. Can you stop by this afternoon?"

Kathy came out of the kitchen and gave John a funny look.

"I suppose."

"You gotta ask permission?"

"No, I'll come over," John said. This seemed like a last chance. A last chance for what, he wasn't sure.

Walter lived in the Center City Apartments, an older building three miles from downtown, but a place that might have been the center a long time ago. John punched a button in the lobby and Walter rang him up. An elevator took him to the sixth floor. Walter was waiting there for him when the elevator door opened. "You might get lost up here," he said.

"Nice building."

"Tom lived in this building."

"Oh, really?"

"Fifth floor, right below me. He used to pound his broom handle on the ceiling when I played the piano. Before we got to know each other."

"I didn't know you played."

"There are a lot of things you don't know." Walter ushered him through the door. The apartment was dark, the drapes tightly closed. Walter clapped twice and turned on a brass, colonial-style lamp.

"Pretty neat."

"Saves me a lot of trouble."

"No piano," John said. "Or maybe one will appear if you clap again."

"Downstairs," Walter said. "It was easier to keep the damn thing in Tom's place."

"I thought he didn't like the sound of your piano." John almost sat on a cat. Hadn't it died? Or maybe Walter owned more than one.

"He just didn't like the sound coming from above him."

"I don't get it."

"Years ago this was—he bought the damn thing from me, a hundred bucks, and then he let me come down to play it whenever I wanted."

"Interesting." John looked at the floor, as if he could see through to Tom's apartment. "And the piano is still down there."

"Well, it's only been a couple months and I haven't had time to get rid of his things, so I just keep paying the rent. I go down there from time to time, to bang out an old song. I enjoy doing that."

"You've been paying his rent?"

"If you really need to know," Walter said, pressing his hands together, "I've been paying his rent for the past three years. You understand?"

"Uh-huh."

"No, you don't understand. I feed his cat now. I'd bring her up here to live with me, but she fights with Sylvia. I had to break up a fight between them. Which is how I scratched my hands that time and you thought I was lying about it." Sylvia jumped into Walter's lap and he rubbed her ears. If this was the cat that had died, then it had managed to resurrect itself.

"What's the other cat's name?"

"Snow White. You wanna see her? I'll get the key."

John figured this had been the original point of the visit—a tour of the dead tenor's apartment. Another memorial service. They took the elevator down to the fifth floor.

Tom's apartment was the exact twin of Walter's, the dark brown furniture identically arranged, a colonial brass lamp in exactly the same place. Walter clapped to make it go on. "Everything works this way," he said, examining his hands. "In both apartments. You clap once for the TV, twice for the lamp. If you don't clap fast enough the TV might go on when all you want is the lamp. You know?"

"Yup."

"But my hands are getting kind of weak to be clapping all the time. Anyway, this is where he lived. It's vacant. You wanna move in?"

"No thanks. I have a place."

"I keep it clean," Walter said. "Every week I come down here and vacuum."

"Where's the cat?"

"Frightened. She probably thinks I'm gonna vacuum. I don't vacuum on Sundays."

"Whose picture is that on the piano?"

"Oh, just me." Walter adjusted the angle on the frame. "Twenty years ago. Wearing a wig. I look thirty, don't I?"

"Yes. Maybe younger."

"Good. Because I was actually thirty-five when it was taken. And now you can do your addition." He flicked his handkerchief at the photo. "This is the only existing copy. And you won't see any other pictures around the place. Tom had several beautiful signed prints hanging in the living room, very valuable, but somebody broke in and stole them."

John picked up a book of art songs from the piano. "What's this?"

"You didn't know it, but a couple years ago, we were thinking about putting on a recital. Tom and I. Three years ago? I forget that sort of thing. We were well into it, and then this happened." He held up his hands. They seemed steady enough.

"What do you mean by 'this'?" John asked.

"The shakes. I have no idea what caused it. Maybe pesticides. I have no idea."

"When did it happen?"

"Gradually, over the past couple years. I lost all control of my fingers. Tom still wanted to put on the recital. He said he'd look for another pianist. We had a horrible fight over it. I told him if he got another pianist, I'd kill him." His right hand knocked against the lampshade. The lamp stayed on.

"Did you?"

"What? No, of course not. He was my best friend. Why would I kill him?"

"I don't know."

"You'll believe anything. I didn't actually tell Tom that I'd kill him. All I said was if he hired another pianist, I wasn't going to pay for it. Now I wish I had. He would have had his recital." Walter played two chords on the piano, minor key. They seemed steady enough. Tender.

"She's a quarter tone flat already. And I just had her tuned." He played the first four notes of "Happy Birthday," then stopped, shook his head. "Last Wednesday was his birthday, you know."

"You told me."

"And I came down here and threw a party. It was just me and Snow White and the spider plant, but that was enough. I turned on the stereo. Snow White sat on my lap and licked my face." He walked over to the bookcase, selected a tape, and put it in the deck. He pressed a button. "We listened to an old tape. This one."

Tenor and piano—simple art songs, probably English. "That's really good," John said. "Tom is the vocalist, right?"

"A long time ago."

"Is that you on the piano?"

"No. It was before we ever met. He was a graduate student in Chicago, back in the sixties. I have no idea who the pianist was. Maybe a girlfriend. There's nothing written on the label—just 'old recital.' See? Tom's handwriting." He set down the case. "If you and I weren't here listening to him, who else would?"

"I never knew Tom very well," John said. "I enjoyed sitting next to him in choir. And I learned a lot from him. He was really solid."

"In contrast to . . ."

"What?"

"In contrast to me, of course."

"I wasn't making any comparisons," John said. "I only meant to say that I thought very well of the guy."

"His life had pretty much wound down to what it was. The apartment, church choir, and, of course, his job at the county building. Seven bucks an hour. He told me he was sleepwalking through everything. He said his life was just an idea, nothing more. It was a surface, with no depth. An image. He didn't put much value on it."

"What did he die of?"

Walter sat down at the piano again and rested his fingers on the keys. The tape stopped. "He died of not wanting to live."

"He was a good singer, at least."

"Yes, good. He was good. Not great. I don't think he wanted to be great. Tom was too lazy to think of building himself up into a great singer and then suffering all the usual disappointments, the rivalry, the insanity. He didn't want that. He didn't think a career as a singer would have made his life any more real than it was."

"Where are his family?"

"And it was hard for him to love. 'The greatest of all things is love,' I told him. I brought him into the church, you know. At least he had that, the church."

"You loved him."

"And I sit here in his apartment sometimes, thinking, asking questions. What is a life? What does death mean? Is death final? The church says I'm supposed to believe it isn't, but my version of immortality is like that character in Kurt Vonnegut. You ever read Kurt Vonnegut?"

"Long time ago."

"In some book by Vonnegut, there's this character who dies. I forget his name. But he dies in a plane crash, I think. It wasn't important. Anyway, he dies, but he's a time traveler, so the fact he dies never affects him much. His character goes back in time. World War Two. He even ends up on a different planet for a while."

"I read that one. Billy Pilgrim."

"My point is," Walter said, "you can take any life and think of it that way. It's a line, and you can move along that line in both directions." He stroked the white keys all the way to the highest note.

"I guess I live in the moment. The present."

"Let me play this for you." He flattened the music, held down the pages with a hymnal on one side and a Cole Porter book on the other. He looked at John as if he expected him to sing. John shook his head. Walter shrugged, played a few bars, then stopped. "Did you feel that?"

"Nice music."

"No, did you feel that?"

"Was there something in the music I was supposed to feel?"

"It's not in the music. Listen again." Walter played four or five chords and stopped again. There was a dull pounding noise. "It's the people underneath, making their opinion known." Walter smiled. "Or person."

"Do you know him? Or her?"

"No. It's a him. I checked the mailbox."

"You could recruit him for the choir," John said. "It worked before."

"A long time ago. We're talking almost twenty years ago." Walter played a sour chord. "I don't want to recruit my replacement. Somebody else can do that, after I'm dead. Which shouldn't be a problem. I'm sure that you, for example, will still be around long after I'm dead. Right?"

"I don't know."

"You will." Then his hands went wild and knocked all the music from the piano. "Oh Lord," he said. "I'm a total wreck."

"Keep playing," John said.

"Oh, you don't wanna hear it."

"Just play something you know by heart. Doesn't matter."

Walter stared at the keys for a minute, then began to play a slow ragtime piece. John watched quietly, standing behind Walter, who seemed so steady while he played, not much older than his real age. When the song was over, John clapped loudly twice, and the light went out. He started to clap some more, to bring the light on again, but decided to leave the room dark.

"No problem," Walter said. "I can play in the dark. Matter of fact, I've been practicing that way, for when I go blind."

"All right, keep playing. I'll listen."

The
Violin

I would just leave, take off with all the apartment windows open. The breeze would carry my papers into the street where children could scavenge among them, and think about me, the guy who used to live up there.

But not today. I sat by the open window and listened to my neighbors pack up and leave—the friendly chatter, the thud of heavy furniture, the implications of every object large and small. The last week in May, the season for moving out, and it wasn't just the students loading U-Hauls, but married women with lovers, whose husbands worked all day and would come home that evening to an emptied house.

Mary and Loverboy. I liked Mary, although I had never met the woman, never said one word to her. She was forty, but didn't look it. With her short dark hair and trim figure, you might have taken her to be the twin brother of Loverboy, who was young enough to be her son. "Loverboy." I made that up, because Mary never said his name, as if she feared that her neighbors would tell her husband. But I wouldn't have. I knew how Rob had abused her, how his voice would press against the walls and shoot out into the night. I knew her name because he had yelled it so many times, and I guessed how old she was from how Rob had made a big deal out of her sneaking out with a boy half her age.

That's how I knew things.

And I wasn't going to stop Mary and Loverboy from emptying the house.

They climbed out of the truck and kissed. They stood in the alley and kissed for two minutes, and then Mary pulled away with a groan. "Stop."

"Why?"

"You're sapping all my strength. We'll never finish in time."

"You're too hung up on furniture. Let's just leave it out here and he'll take care of it. I got plenty. Just leave it, okay?"

"Some of this stuff belonged to my mother."

"What does that mean? Is that important?" His voice sounded high, adolescent, lacking in some essential confidence. Was he even through high school?

"My mother is dead."

"So, what's the problem?"

"I don't know," she said.

"I don't, either. I mean, so is mine and look how young I am." Mary might have looked. I didn't.

"Sorry. I shouldn't of said that. You look young, too," he said softly. "And hey—you already decorated my place real nice for me. Wall hangings and pillows and stuff. You're comfortable with it, right?"

"Yeah."

"What else do you need?" he asked.

"Nothing."

"So you're cleaning out the house to piss him off. That's all this is."

"Yeah."

"I just wanted to clarify that."

"Is that okay?"

"It's the best reason I can think of, Mary." They kissed again, briefly, touching their lips at first, then closing in for complete contact. Mary and her lover were exactly the same height; they fit together as if they had been sculpted by the same artist.

Loverboy pulled away and leaned against the wall. "You almost suffocated me," he said.

"Sorry."

"That's okay. So we just take what we got in the truck, and then leave. Do we got something of your mother's already packed on the truck? If we did, then you could stop crying about it and we could clear out before that asshole gets back from work."

"I don't know."

I really did not want to see them kiss again, so I lay back in bed and listened. There was the sound of heavy objects being tossed around in an empty room—wood, metal. Not skin and bones. I liked this sound. Then Mary and Loverboy came out again. I heard the door slap.

"Okay," Mary said. "Let's dump this awful couch out in the alley somewhere. It stinks from his cigarettes."

"The cloth is in shreds. I sure don't want it."

"It's that damn cat. We should have declawed him, but Rob, you know how he is about animals."

"I don't know."

"He said it would be cruel. Now the cat runs wild, never comes home. Where is he, anyway?" She started calling out, "Agatha? Agatha?"

"He's named Agatha?"

"He, she, it. Does it matter?"

"Just wondered where the name came from."

"We inherited the cat, name and all. I have no idea."

I knew. I could have shouted the answer from my window. I knew the people who had lived there before Rob and Mary. I'd even talked with them once or twice. They'd told me how they had named the cat before they figured out its sex, and how it kept coming home beat up, so they took it to the vet and found out Agatha was a tomcat. They had it neutered, but kept the name Agatha. Loverboy and Mary could not have stood still for such an explanation, from the upstairs window of a stranger who would not show his face.

They went in the house and rattled around, and the acoustics improved. The curtains must have been down by that point.

Loverboy stood in the doorway holding a black case. "How about this? It looks pretty old."

"God," Mary said, "it's my old violin!"

"I thought it was a banjo case. I tried to play a banjo once and it hurt my damn fingers."

"That violin! God!"

"Don't cry, Mary."

"I'm laughing!"

It sounded like crying to me. I knew the way she cried. I'd heard enough of it the past month through my open window. Her cry was three-toned, regular, always the same, like a bird call. And when she could get it out, the entire bird call, only then would the shouting stop, and we'd have peace in the neighborhood.

"I know the way you cry," Loverboy said. "You're crying. So, you wanna keep the violin? Or not?"

She waited a moment. "Does that ever bring back memories."

"You play it?"

"I've completely forgotten how. I haven't seen that awful violin since we moved here five years ago. I played in college, I think. I guess. God."

"Well, let's take your violin out of the case and see how much you remember."

"That's sadistic."

"Come on."

"Oh, Jesus, no," she said. "Please. We're wasting time. He may get home any minute."

"I'll hide while you play." He kind of laughed when he said that.

She laughed, too, with a snort. "That's not it. Rob would know something was going on just to hear the violin."

"He doesn't like it?"

"No, it's just, the music would raise certain expectations."

"Of?"

She lowered her voice. "Let's just dump it."

"No way. It's illegal to throw out a violin."

"That's crazy. What do you know about it?"

"I just know." Loverboy opened the violin case and held up the instrument. "Hey, look, it doesn't even have no strings on it or nothing. I was gonna ask you to play. I mean, I was really gonna make you do it."

"You don't make me do things."

"Sure I do," he said, and leaned to kiss her again.

"He probably ripped them out." She looked over her shoulder. "Anyway, it's better without the strings. Safer."

Absolute silence, some traffic far away, air conditioners humming, a faint ringing in my ears. I swallowed to get rid of the ringing, and now there was complete quiet. There wasn't going to be any music. Safer. No strings.

"Let's get moving," she said.

"Did you have a favorite tune?"

"No. I hated it," she said. "Let's get moving."

"Hated what?"

"Any kind of music. I did it to please my mother." She laughed. It wasn't that pathetic bird call, but something deep in the chest.

"Well, I like some kinds of music," he said. "I always liked Irish music."

"You would."

"Something wrong with Irish music?"

"I didn't say that."

"You like the English?"

"I'm not English," she said.

"Italian."

"I'm not Italian. That's my married name."

"Rub it in."

"I have nothing against Irish music," she said. "I just don't know any."

I cleared my throat. I knew several Irish songs, and could have performed them. I could have gotten out of bed and sung to Mary and Loverboy from my open window. After all, they were moving, and without much ceremony. They deserved a proper ceremony. Again, I cleared my throat, but I had no voice that day, and couldn't break through into their separate universe.

"Mary," the boy said softly.

"Yes?"

"I want to sing something to you right here, but I'll forget the words. I hate to start a song and then stop right in the middle."

"It would be illegal, right?"

"Right!" he laughed.

"And we don't want to do anything illegal."

"They'd put us in jail."

"Don't talk like that," she said.

"Come on, Mary. I was just kidding."

"Right."

"Please, let me sing. Please?" He sounded ten years old.

"We can wait until we get to your place, then you can sing all you want."

"I'll forget even more of them."

"All right, go ahead. Nobody is listening."

And then Loverboy sang an Irish ballad—"King William." A real folk song, unaccompanied. The queen and some knave had betrayed King William, stabbed him in the back while he slept. "All in the month of May," the refrain went, which made me smile. Loverboy sang while he worked. He had a good untrained voice, and the singing evidently gave him strength, as he loaded another dresser onto the back of the truck without skipping a beat. Loverboy was still going strong when they drove away. I could hear him launch into a tenth verse. Mary was laughing. And whatever Loverboy sang, the notes kept coming after the words dissolved into the intervening trees and buildings.

All in the month of May.

I sat up in bed. I stood and went to the window and looked down into the alley. They had left the violin out of its case, propped against one arm of the discarded couch. I wanted it. There was a place in town that could put new strings on that violin and sell me a bow. And although I had no voice, I knew some beautiful music that I could eventually learn to play.

Two Altos

HELEN AND MARIAN

Helen points her coffee cup at her sister-in-law. "That woman can't stop talking. I swear to God. She always has to finish her story. In church, even. She just can't shut up when the choir director yells, 'Quiet!' She touches my arm when I turn away from her to pick up my music, and she says, 'Don't you dare. I'm not finished. Listen to what I'm saying, Helen, and don't sing a note until I finish my sentence. Anyway, I have to give you your note.' That's Marian for you. Thinks she knows everything about music, always picks the worst possible time for a conversation, and blames me for hitting the wrong note. But how can I get it right when she's talking like that? You tell me."

Marian doesn't bother to look at Helen. She keeps busy wiping her kitchen counters, which, of course, don't need to be wiped. "Always making fun. 'Oh, I'm twelve years younger. I'm still pretty. I lead a more interesting life. I get out and dance.' Well, let me tell you, looks aren't everything. I went to conservatory and took voice lessons. Helen never did. She smokes and can't sing without gasping for air. I won't let her smoke here in my kitchen, though. My kitchen is off-limits. She has to behave herself in here." Marian sits down and sighs. "Sometimes after she comes for a visit, an hour later I can smell the smoke blowing in the window, and I find the cigarette butts out on the lawn. That's Helen."

"Wait a minute. Don't listen to her. I haven't touched a cigarette in twenty years." Helen taps her long red nails on the formica table.

"What's that for?"

"What's what for?"

"Tap, tap, tap. Deaf, too. Helen always had to go out dancing. All that loud rock music took away her hearing."

"You know, this is what really happened," Helen says, still tapping. "I worked in a factory for many years. If I lost any of my hearing, and I don't think I have, it was from that racket in the mill. They didn't have protective headphones back then. Now I'm paying the price—if she says I'm deaf. I admit that I have a slight hearing loss. I do the best I can with what I have."

"Helen, look at your hands. You're tapping your fingers right now and you can't even hear it. Lord almighty, it's impossible for me to think straight when you're tapping out messages like that. Tap, tap, tap. She's communicating with her dead ancestors. That's what she does. She's telling them, here I come, I'm all ready to die." Marian gets up from her chair with a grunt, and takes the teakettle off the burner. "Helen is much older than she looks. She's not particularly healthy, what with all the cigarettes and caffeine."

"Don't be ridiculous. This started out when Marian's husband Charlie—my big brother—he had his heart attack two years ago, and then of course, he died, and old Marian, with Charlie dead and all, she needed a free ride to choir and to church and every other place in town. I took pity on her. I became her driver, for free. That was all. I never pretended to be the singer in this family."

"Hah!"

"Marian was always very dependent on Charlie. She never learned how to drive. Never worked. Her parents spent all that money for her conservatory training and it turned out she never even gave one piano lesson, for all the money they invested in her. She should be in there now dusting off those piano keys."

Marian pours the hot water so that Helen's cup overflows onto the table.

Helen lifts her perfect fingertips so as not to touch the overflow. "My God. Blind. She's going blind. Good thing I'm here to do for her. You know? She could never pass the eye test for her driver's license. She couldn't get past line one." Helen looks at her sister-in-law. "Deaf and blind. What a pair. That should help you to keep us straight."

Marian folds a paper towel on top of the spill. "All of this started with Charlie's heart attack, and then he died and left me by myself. It's been hard for me." She gets another paper towel and rubs until the table is dry. "Helen never married—that we know of. Life was very empty for her, no family. I have two daughters but they both moved to another state. Anyway, Helen said she wanted to join the choir. I knew she couldn't sing, so I said, 'Just come and listen, my dear. Listen and learn. Eventually, if you think you can handle the music, maybe then you can come up and join us.' And she did, after two months or so. Before she was ready, in my opinion. Just came up and sat next to me in the alto section and started grabbing my music away from me. To listen to Helen, you'd think it would have been better for her to go over and sing with the tenors or basses. She had quite a struggle singing middle C. Isn't that something? Everyone can sing middle C. That's the note we yawn on. That's the note where all the voices come together. In many pieces of music, all four parts are given that same note, and they spread out from there. But Helen is already spread out, singing the bass clef. They'd welcome her over there, in the bass section, those dirty old men. Church choir has become much too social, in my opinion."

"I'm pretty good now. Tom says he'll give me a solo."

The remark is so outrageous, Marian simply looks out the window. The mailman should come soon. She expects a package from a half-size company that specializes in pantsuits.

"Marian, I said Tom wants me to sing a solo. Look at her. Trying to act like she doesn't care. Is that a jealous woman or what?"

"The truth changes every time you open your mouth," Marian says.

"You are really out of it, lady."

"When did Tom say anything about you singing a solo? He has never said anything to you that I didn't hear. And he never gave you a solo. Never. He'd have to be crazy. There are fifteen people—at least—ahead of you in line to do a solo. Maybe Tom was telling Herman that he had a solo and you thought he was saying Helen."

"Nonsense. Every rehearsal—this is funny—Marian makes two trips to the bathroom. Bladder trouble, you know, probably because she always brings that thermos of tea with her, which is half sugar and very unhealthy. Not during a break, but right in the middle of

something, Marian just dashes off to the bathroom. She's in there
five minutes sometimes, and we just go on with the rehearsal. We
can't wait for her. Tom gave me a solo while Marian was in the bathroom last Thursday night. He said, 'I want you to look at this solo,
take it home and study it and see what you think,' which means I will
eventually sing that solo in church, doesn't it? Why else would he tell
me to look at it?" Helen begins to tap her fingers again, in waltz
tempo, a mischievous smile on her face.

"What are you tapping?"

"My solo."

"Oh, that's ridiculous."

"I'm learning the rhythm. Tom said to tap it out whenever I had
the chance."

"What are the words, Helen?"

"Oh, I don't know. Who cares? Tom and I will get to the words eventually, I'm sure. I may start going over to church on Tuesday nights.
He wants to see me extra hours, he said. To work on my top notes."

"Tuesday nights!"

"Oh, don't worry, Marian, you don't have to come along. You can
stay home in your bathrobe. I won't be stopping by to pick you up. It'll
just be Tom and me."

"This just gets worse and worse. The lying. Charlie was bad, but not
this bad. It ran in the family." Marian whispers, "Their mother—who
would be ninety-eight if she were still alive—said she was fourth
cousin of the Queen Mother. A lie if I ever heard one. Look at Princess
Helen. She probably didn't hear that remark with all her tapping. Tap,
tap, tap. Tap, tap, tap."

"You're throwing me off, Marian. You never had good rhythm. I'll
sing the words for you next week. Think you can wait that long?"

"There are other stories, other stories. Wait till you hear the really
good ones."

"She makes them up. Marian says I don't tell the truth? Just wait.
She lives in a world of make-believe. Marian supposedly sang in an
opera. Chicago Lyric Opera, before she got married. I can just imagine. She might have played a donkey."

"Get out! Get out now!"

MARIAN

Marian wears a new lime green pantsuit. She brushes cake crumbs from the lapels. "My sister-in-law isn't here tonight. Didn't even stay for tea. Didn't get out of the car, or even really stop the car to let me out. I almost took a fall in the gravel, and she wouldn't have even known. I called out her name and she drove off without saying anything. She had to hurry home, tires squealing. For what? Some TV show that she's been watching since the beginning of the decade. We were supposed to rehearse another half hour, but Helen vetoed that pretty fast. Stood up and put on her coat, and Tom said, 'Well, I guess that's it for tonight.' It really frightens me how much power that woman has accumulated. In less than a year of being in the choir. Without being able to sing!" Marian pours a cup of tea for herself, slices another piece of bundt cake from the pan. "The sugar won't hurt me. I'll go to bed happy."

She looks out the dark window, as if she can still see the taillights from Helen's Nova, though everything is gray to her. "She won't. Don't think I hate her or resent her. I would not have done all I have for that woman if I did not love her like my own sister. And pity her. I think pity is the right word for it. Fifty-five years old and never been married. We always had her over, for the holidays and different occasions, like when the girls graduated high school. We always tried to include her in our life. Now it's pathetic to watch her try to make up for lost time. The painted fingernails. The hair. The low-cut dresses. The perfume! It makes me gag, sitting next to that woman. But I really have to hand it to Helen. She is very loyal to the choir, and she makes the effort. Her singing has improved slightly. Her range has increased by one octave and she can almost read music now. The notes. It's the rhythm that she can't figure out. She always wants to put a snappy beat on everything. She's always snapping her fingers, as if we should pick up the tempo. But that's her shortness of breath. If we drag it out too long, she might just choke and die. That's what cigarettes will do to you."

Marian finishes the last of her cake and debates whether she'll go for a third piece. She sweeps the crumbs into the palm of her hand and flings them into her mouth. "Sunday morning. This is funny. Well, you know she's six inches taller than me. Add on all that ridiculous hair and the spike heels and make it a foot. Well, Sunday morning she couldn't find her robe. So she grabs mine instead. We have the same last name, which is written on the inside label. Robertson. She ought to be able to tell she has the wrong robe on. My robe hardly comes down to her knees. And all she has on is this short dress, several inches above the knees. Some of the men start whistling at her. And there I am standing in my pantsuit with no robe, while she models my robe for all the men, twirling around this way and that, like some dance hall floozie. We were late for the first hymn because of all the nonsense. Tom doesn't care. He just laughs at that kind of thing. He's the worst of them."

HELEN

"Oh Lord, you wouldn't believe it. During church service Marian grabbed my arm and spit in my ear. She said, 'Helen, I'm gonna learn to drive before you kill me going a hundred miles an hour on River Road.' I took out my handkerchief and wiped the spit from my ear and then folded it and put it back in my purse. I didn't say anything. I was listening to the sermon, or trying to. I can't figure what her learning to drive has to do with anything. Maybe she wants to follow me around at night. She has nothing better to do with her life. She tells me she hates singing in the choir now. She may even quit. I ask her what the choir would do without her."

MARIAN

"Helen hasn't done any solos yet. Thank the Lord. We haven't even practiced anything with a solo part in it for Helen. I asked Tom to set out all the music for the rest of the year, so I could get a head start, which was not true. I don't need a head start. I sight-read everything.

"So Tom had a long table of new music laid out in the choir room, and I loaded up my folder after rehearsal. Nothing had a solo for Helen. Or for me, a trained singer. I've been in this choir at Bethlehem Methodist so long people forget that I have a trained voice. I could sing loud, opera-like, but I'd rather blend with the other singers. I sing loud enough to give the notes to Helen, since she still cannot read them.

"At the conservatory I was more outgoing than I am now. I met several famous composers who taught there or came for a visit. I own signed copies of everything Randall Thompson ever wrote. I have a beautiful signed copy of 'Alleluia' hidden in that old desk. Now, I ask you, what choir has never sung that piece? You're right—Bethlehem Methodist has never pulled it out of the filing cabinet, in spite of my subtle hints. Tom once admired my signed copy, which I brought to rehearsal. He said, 'Put it away someplace where it will be safe, where your sister won't rip it out of your hands.' Then he laughed. I told him, 'It's not funny. And she's not my sister.' "

Marian's hands shake. Nothing she grabs is steady enough.

HELEN

"Tom and I drove down by the river that Tuesday night, past the Norseland Supper Club? They were advertising all you could eat for five dollars. I was starved.

" 'Are you hungry?' He touched my arm the way he does every time he says something to me.

" 'No, of course not.'

" 'Singing doesn't make you hungry?'

" 'No, not really. Tom, darling, do you mind if I smoke?' He doesn't mind—he lets me do anything.

"I rolled down the window just a little ways and the sweet smell of apple blossoms flowed into the car. I decided not to smoke, as a special favor to him. We stopped at the overlook. Across the river, the radio towers throbbed with red light. My heart beat in rhythm with those lights.

" 'Really,' he said. 'Go ahead and smoke. I won't mind.'

" 'It's not good for my voice.'

" 'When can we talk about your solo?' he asked. If I hadn't been paying close attention to the individual words, I would have thought he was suggesting I take off my clothes. And don't I wish!

"I turned to him and said, 'Are you only interested in music? You're just like my sister-in-law. Her life revolves around her church music. The rest of the week she goes into suspended animation. I suppose you didn't know that.'

" 'She's very loyal.'

" 'If Marian didn't have choir to look forward to every week, she'd probably die. I have to give her rides all the time. I hate dependent people.'

"   'Nobody depends on me. So I'm neutral.'
"   'Is that why you got rid of your wife?'
"   'I've never been married.'
"   'Why not?'
"   'Music.'
"   'Music? My God, not that excuse again!'
"   'But Helen,' he said, 'I need to talk to you about your solo.' He gripped my hand. I told him to wait. Did we ever talk about it? Did I let him change the subject? Hell, I knew the score. There wasn't going to be a solo. Not in church anyway, not with my awful voice. In his house, sure. He had a nice piano sitting there in its own little room—no curtains, no carpeting, no pictures on the wall. He sat at the piano and I guess eventually I sang."

Quartet

Soprano

She wore a surgical mask to choir rehearsal, believing that the other sopranos might infect her. She caught a bad cold in spite of the mask and screwed up her big solo that Sunday, ears too plugged to hear the organ.

Alto

One day, her head was so clear that she began to think anything was possible—she could swim ten miles, climb a tree, punch a hole in the wall, sing a hundred measures without breathing.

Tenor

He poked at his ears for an hour. He was drowning in ambient noise. This was a slow death—painless for now, although pain would eventually come.

Bass

He held his stomach while he sang a very low note, felt it vibrate in his hand, and thought, "This is obscene." He smiled until sunset.

Soprano

"You keep getting a cold because you keep singing in your throat," her teacher said, looking away from her. "You've got to stop doing that."

Where else could she sing? Everything about singing was such a mystery. "Tell me what you mean, Elizabeth."

"I want you to sing in the mask, darling."

"What?"

"You need to sing in the mask."

"Show me. Turn around. Show me how."

"I'm sorry, darling, but you have to think about it first. No singing without thinking." Elizabeth touched her own forehead, which was about the size of a postage stamp. Her mask. "Think of how you could be like a garbage truck. All the garbage inside vibrating and rattling."

"What?" She hated the weird comparisons that her teacher always came up with. A truck? What could be uglier?

"It's an excellent way to loosen up and sing right."

"Show me."

Elizabeth leaned back, shook her wild black hair, and grunted, producing an inhuman noise that grew louder and louder and then ended on a high shriek. She sounded insane. Maybe she was. She spun around, clutched her throat, fell to the floor, and lay there motionless, her long black skirt twisted around her thin legs.

"Are you okay?"

"I scared you." She opened her eyes and smiled.

"Almost. I thought you were possessed."

"Possessed! That's good. I hope it sounded like the devil." Elizabeth stood and brushed off her skirt. "This exercise is right for me. It helps me to place my voice properly. It saves my voice. When I sang the lead in Saratoga Light Opera, remember, last fall? I was Princess Ida, with all those high notes above the staff, and my voice was so tight?" Elizabeth always turned the conversation toward her own career.

"How would it save my voice?"

"It would break down the false protection, the little compensations that are destructive to good singing."

"I never knew that."

"If we could regress to infancy, or go back a few steps in evolution, we wouldn't have all these problems." Elizabeth seemed to be suggesting that the apes were better singers. Or frogs. That made more sense.

"I'll try anything."

"I like that about you."

"Well, I'm desperate. You have no idea."

So they spent the next fifteen minutes grunting together, side by side on the floor. Thirty dollars an hour for that. For that, the soprano thought, I could hire a pig, real cheap.

"What are you thinking about, darling? We don't have any secrets in this studio."

"My mind's a complete blank."

"That's it!" Elizabeth grabbed her by the shoulders, kissed her on the cheek. "That's it! Exactly! Empty your mind. Blank it out. Then sing!"

"Now?"

"Sorry, dear. Not now." She stood up and kicked her rug back into place. "I have to get ready for Mona."

"But she doesn't come for another hour."

"I have to meditate, darling."

"Does that help?"

"If you do it right. I always meditate before a performance. Last month, when I was singing Mimi . . ."

ALTO

Folk music. Celtic. She turned off the radio. She liked the sound, but it reminded her of a missed opportunity twenty years ago, two guys with black hair who were taking poetry with her, names forgotten, and Julia, her best friend—the four of them sitting on the lawn in front of the Old Library, warm weather, the sun just setting. A couple of songs, a great blend, and then nothing. Zero. Oh, maybe a dirty look from her friend whenever they passed each other between classes, after Julia had switched her major from English to sociology and moved off campus, discovered nonintersecting paths. Her memory of it was composed in black and white—generic faces and clothes and furniture. The voices of the other three singers blurred into a soft chord from which she could not pick out any single part. Her own voice seemed separate, excluded, out of tune.

She adjusted to the quiet of her place, broken only by the rowboat rubbing against the dock. Even in late fall, she liked the rub-rub sound, semiregular, almost noteless. It reminded her of how inaccessible she was—nine miles by ferry from the mainland and three thousand miles from her mother, Virginia, who, unfortunately, had her number programmed into her phone and could break through the isolation by pressing a single button. A good reason to keep the phone unplugged.

She loved the sound of her boat, and wanted to turn up the volume, the music it made when it slapped the water, knocked against the soft, rotting wood. Any other music carried risks.

TENOR

He hummed while he worked, put a melody to the banal legal texts with which he was daily confronted.

The rest of the office didn't mind. They complimented him on his voice, asked him to put the actual words to the melody, as if these were real songs. He would frown and say, "I can't remember them." But at an office party, the tenor sang a couple of tunes from *Brigadoon* and *My Fair Lady,* from memory, no mistakes, and a woman said, "In your other life, before you moved out here to Minneapolis, you must have been a musician. You sang opera, didn't you?"

"Oh, I might have dreamed of it. Nothing more."

"I'm sure it was more than a dream. Are you interested in performing a duet with me?" Her voice was golden and smooth. He knew he could blend with her.

"Are you talking about music?"

"What do you think?"

"Well, if it's just music, then maybe," he said. But "maybe" wasn't good enough, and she found another tenor. Everything he sang was solo, although sometimes in his mind, other voices would coil around his, sinuous and demanding.

BASS

He loved to chant. He would chant alone if he absolutely had to. It changed the geography for a few minutes, took him out of Schenectady, out of this dead time in his life—too many mornings and afternoons spent in front of the television, or in front of the mirror, with the light turned off.

SOPRANO

She seldom sang when by herself, always needed an audience, couldn't trust her own ears.

ALTO

She loved to chant, alone.

TENOR

He dropped by his office on a Sunday after church. Something from his sister on e-mail, a message sent late Saturday afternoon. She got right to the point: "I am leaving my marriage. Big shock to you, probably, so it's a good thing you're sitting down. A shock to me, too, since I didn't see it coming. Bob and I looked like we'd just make do with the situation forever, at least keep the monster alive until our twentieth. Now it's dead, and he has to be out of here by the first of December. Don't ask what the monster died of. So tell me, dear brother—what are you doing this year for Christmas? Can you come to Schenectady?"

I'm doing nothing. I'm not even singing in church.

But he held his fingers away from the keyboard, tapped on the mouse pad, something in alternating triples and duples. He would have to compose the perfect reply—a sentence or a paragraph that he would work out on paper first, longhand.

Kathy was lonely, and not afraid to tell him. She must have had women friends she could talk to—friends at work and from church. Not him. He was no good for listening. When people came to him with their problems, he tended to go blank, fade into the static. So he wouldn't call her.

He turned on the radio. Barbershop. He turned it off.

BASS

He loved to chant—English or Latin, Anglican or plainsong, it didn't matter. He loved the rise and fall, the natural rhythm, the blending of voices, separate and very different lives coming together in perfect octaves. But that kind of perfection never lasted. Some fool always wrecked it. Petty disputes, jealousies, sudden illnesses, church politics. He knew this from forty years of choir singing.

And so when his chant-loving choir director was fired and most of the choir resigned, and he was left alone with two guys on guitar and three sopranos who couldn't read music, he decided to hang up his robe, walk out the door, and never come back. He would sleep late on Sunday mornings until he died.

Sunday mornings, he would play the chant album and eat his breakfast—toasted English muffins, spread thick with marmalade, a stack of buttermilk pancakes, half a dozen sausages. Sunday mornings, he had been strict about what he ate, because he had cared how he sang. But for a whole month, he stuffed his face and lay in bed, sick to his stomach, belching, hating himself.

On a gray Monday after he had phoned his broker and shifted eighty thousand dollars into new accounts, he drove into the city looking for another church. He parked at several without getting out of the car. Something would be obviously wrong—roof pitched too low, bell tower made of aluminum, dog vomiting on the sidewalk.

St. Paul's Methodist had a black-and-white sign that read *Visitors Park Here. Welcome. And God Bless You.* No tow-away threats with apostrophe errors. So he parked, sat in the car for a minute and looked at the church. The exterior was stone Gothic, which made him think he could make good music in there, loosen up everything that had tightened, regain some of the pleasure he had lost.

The door was open. He wiped his shoes on a welcome mat in the narthex and sat in one of the rear pews, stared straight ahead at a pink-and-amber stained glass abstraction, and sent his voice toward the ceiling in warm-up syllables, a couple of tentative doobie-doos that stretched into a plainsong chant on nonsense syllables. The notes came back to him exactly as he had imagined them, and better than he had sung them.

"Hello, hello, hello," he sang, before leaving.

"Who's that?" a woman shouted as he went out the door.

The first few weeks at St. Paul's Methodist he sat with the congregation, second pew from the back, and sang along on the hymns. He would belt out the melody when the organ played loud—at least the high notes; some low notes were unsingable. All the hymns went like that, as if the Methodists had transposed the Episcopal hymnal down a whole tone or more. Sometimes they actually expected the basses to sing a low E, like that guy Larry Hooper on the Lawrence Welk show. An E-flat!

He could not compete with the Larry Hoopers of the bass world.

Low E-flat was possible only between six and six-thirty in the morning, in a semiconscious state. By the time he had taken his morning shower, the E-flat had dissolved and a low G had become his effective bottom—not just a raspy grunt, but a note on which he could resonate and make each vowel different. And if he fiddled with the G too much, he would lose that note, too. Without the G, he felt less of a man. Every note lost from the bottom of his range was an erosion of his manhood.

SOPRANO

She stepped through the beaded curtains into the studio, where her teacher lay on the dirty floor, eyes shut. "Elizabeth, are you all right?"

Elizabeth opened her eyes and sat up, yoga-style. "You're frowning," she said, clinically. "Frowning is very bad for singing. It distorts the mask, and that's where bad vowels come from."

"I know. You told me."

"So what's the problem this week, darling?"

"They've decided to stop paying me!" She threw her hands in the air, made an arch around her head. "Sunday was my last payday! Help!"

"Everybody's hurting."

"This church sure isn't. You should see these people, the furs they wear, the diamonds. Loaded with money. Millionaires. Maybe even a billionaire."

"Really?"

"Really."

"Then I should sing there, find a wealthy man to support me. Okay, now I want you to smile." Elizabeth stood up. She smiled and nodded her head quickly, as if to demonstrate how. "Do it for me. Right now, darling, your whole face. Before it's too late."

She grimaced. "They had no reason to cut me off like that." She tossed her suede jacket on the couch. "Maybe I'm too old. Am I?"

"You're not old," Elizabeth said. "Here, let me massage your neck."

"They think I'm not worth the money, all of a sudden."

"How old are you?"

"I'm fifty-five." She paused while Elizabeth examined her face, framed it with her soft hands. "Really."

"You take wonderfully good care of yourself. I'm amazed. You're so pretty."

"Over the hill. It's all downhill from this point. What am I taking lessons for?"

"You seem young even to have teenage children," Elizabeth said. "Maybe forty, I would have guessed. A very young forty."

"I'm old enough to have teenage grandchildren, for God's sake." Her lower back ached. She needed a full back rub. Elizabeth could do that for her, twenty dollars an hour, but her fingers were too soft. "Oh, Elizabeth, I feel terrible. I can't sing anymore. I'm finished!"

"It's just a cold, darling."

"I wish I were immune. Colds make me suicidal."

"You'll get over it."

"Luckily, I'm such a coward that I never go beyond thinking about suicide. I don't ever make specific plans."

"You'll get over it."

"Give me some hope."

"Okay. When you're on, you're great. I mean it. Age is irrelevant. Stop crying now. There's a reason for everything. They'll regret it, and you won't. You'll find something better. I know you will. Please don't cry, darling."

"I thought crying was good for singing."

"Did I say that?"

"Last week."

"If I said it, then it's true. It worked for me at some point in my career. I've certainly cried enough." They sat on the couch and talked for the rest of the hour, on topics ranging from numerology to school board politics. At the end of the lesson, the soprano took out her purse and paid her teacher.

ALTO

She hadn't smoked in six months. Her lungs felt good. Her lips were soft. Her cough was gone.

Still, the high notes wouldn't come. The notes had perched on a stepladder, all the same, shaped like pom-poms with little white triangular flags sticking out from the top. She imagined the clear high notes forming in her throat, leaping into the air, unburdened by bad times, bad habits, bad vibes. But imagining them wasn't enough.

She could go to a doctor, a throat specialist, ask for an operation to undo the damage from smoking and singing too hard and talking wrong. A Teflon implant. It would cost a fortune, and she had no medical coverage.

Mornings when it didn't rain, she jogged on the one-lane gravel road that circled the island. She ran wearing her headphones, playing a tape of the Spanish monks—*Chant Noël*. She could sing quite comfortably in their octave, and she liked blending with the monks and imagined they might feel the same way about her. The words didn't matter; they could have been satanic. Although she had often sung in Latin, she didn't know what the words meant, beyond the obvious ones like "Deus." It was just a good language for singing about God, simple consonants and clear vowels.

TENOR

"So, Kathy," he replied on e-mail, three days later, fingers shaking slightly, some letters repeating. "The big D, huh? I hardly know what to say. Need a place to hide out from him? You should visit me in Minneapolis." He paused and looked out the window. The office building opposite his window was dripping with bird crap. "Plenty of room in the apartment. For example, I have one room with nothing but a piano in it—not that you would have to sleep there. The spare bedroom is all made up, with a mint on the pillow. You could take a bereavement leave. Tell them your brother died. Ha-ha." He sent it.

Two minutes later, the computer beeped. New mail. "Bad joke. Dead brothers are nothing to laugh about. The fact is, it would be really hard to leave town, even for a few days. Not because I can't take off from work—I'm not that busy. The reason is, I don't trust Bob. If he drove by and didn't see any lights on, he'd take stuff that doesn't belong to him."

He sent a three-word reply. "Change the locks."

"Schenectady—for Christmas. Take off a few days."

"I'd get in the way, Kathy. I'll stay here and we can visit on the Internet. It's much simpler, don't you think?"

"No! I need to see you, touch you, confirm that you're a real person. You'll sleep in Bob's room. He had his own room. And I'll clean it, finally. If you move in, then Bob won't be hanging around, sponging meals off me, making me do his laundry, pay his bills. You don't take up much space. In fact, you're too thin."

"I'll get back to you on this."

"We should talk. Bob is gone most of the time. He won't be listening in, unless he tapped the line, but he'd never go to the trouble." They sent messages back and forth a dozen times that afternoon. They were both in their offices, with no outside life. He worried about Kathy, that she had a fake job in that insurance office, the kind where you sit at your desk pretending you're busy—coffee breaks and paper shuffling and frequent phone calls to get the time and temperature. E-mail.

Pavarotti blasted from the office radio. Physically painful. He switched to a bluegrass station. The music felt good, gave him a lift. Then he logged off and stared at the bookcase, the gray coffee mug his old girlfriend had given him—the notes for "Jingle Bells" printed on it in green and red, only the first two measures, in a bad key, which annoyed him, because when he looked at the mug, he started to hum the tune in that key. He had perfect pitch. If he saw musical notes on the page—or on a coffee mug—in a particular key, that key became fixed in his mind.

A thousand years from now, musicologists would reconstruct the entire song from those two measures, or they would look at the notes and assume that they were abstract representations of human beings, making love or fighting.

Bass

His former church placed an advertisement in the *Daily Gazette*, illustrated by a random string of notes that had cartoon faces drawn on them. "Volunteer singers needed for folk choir." So the guitars had won, and the congregation would be strumming and yodeling through the Gloria and Sanctus. He would never go back. He crossed himself, to seal the promise.

Soprano

When she dropped off Tara at ballet practice downtown, there was a poster in the lobby, hot pink, with red script lettering and a crude sketch of a man and woman dancing, both in kilts. Saratoga Light Opera Company was auditioning "trained singers" for their chorus. In four months they would be putting on *Brigadoon*. The poster really should have been plaid around the border, in green and earth tones. They should have used a photo of authentic dancers.

"My time is too valuable for you," she said, tapping her finger on the poster, directly on the face of the woman dancer. "You want trained singers, but you won't pay them! Just forget it!" She knew how SLOC would perform the show—with untrained singers wearing microphones and a prerecorded accompaniment.

Sunday morning, instead of singing with the choir, she wore a big hat with a veil and secluded herself in a back pew of her church, next to an old couple who seemed completely frozen—eyes closed, jaws open, skin colorless. During a prayer the man reached out and grabbed his wife's hand. The wife squeezed back with an iron grip. They still connected at that single point, where their hands met, if nowhere else, and one couldn't help thinking that blood flowed between them, through that connection, and brain waves, and even a bit of music.

On the last hymn, the man took a hymnal from the holder and opened it to the wrong page. While everybody else sang, the old couple sat and looked at the wrong music, and were still looking at it after the hymn was over. That's no life, she thought. When I'm that far gone, I want to be dead.

She saved her voice. If Holy Redeemer Church would not pay her, then there was no reason to sit up front with that damned choir. To hell with them. Without her voice, the sopranos would screw up—she would find out how badly in ten or fifteen minutes when they sang the offertory. They would miss all their entrances, sing flat, cough, fumble their music, giggle when they made mistakes. On Monday, she would report back to Elizabeth, and they would spend the entire hour talking about her old choir and various other bad things that threw the world off balance.

ALTO

For a year she had belonged to a barbershop quartet. Sweet Adelines. She sang bass, and sounded like a man. On the tape, it sounded weird, the voice of a stranger. Macho man. She often played it while jogging.

When people called asking if she would switch to MCI or try the Discover Card or answer questions for a political survey, she would take a deep breath and tell them, "Sorry, not today," and they would ask, "May I speak with your wife?"

"My wife is dead," she would answer, and then hang up. Or, "We're divorced."

"It's Virginia," her mother said, calling for the second time that week. "I was sure I had the wrong number. These days, I often misdial. You really do sound like a man."

"Is that so bad?"

"Do you look like a man?"

"Why do you ask?"

"You never dress up. Your hair's always so short. You're wearing pants right now, aren't you?"

She was wearing black tights and a gray sweatshirt. She touched her hair. It was okay, one inch long all over, clean and smooth, perfect. "I have no mirrors in this place."

"No mirrors? That sounds very strange to me. How on earth can you tell what you look like?"

"It doesn't matter. The cat doesn't care." In fact, the cat had clawed at her tights that morning, ripping them in several places.

"And that's it. You and the cat?"

"Right now, yes, that's it. Me and the cat and a couple of elderly spider plants. They don't care either. Okay?"

"Anything you do is okay with me, really. You don't have to hide anything from me."

"I wish that were true."

"It is. Now listen, honey, I want you to come and visit me for Christmas. The whole family will be there."

"You and me and who else?"

"We'll go to church," Virginia continued. "I'm still in the choir. They haven't fired me yet! We have a lovely choir."

"I'm sure. Why would they fire you?"

"I'm not much of a singer."

"You're a fine singer, Mother."

"Not like you. We'll sing Christmas carols together."

"I don't know."

"What's keeping you on that island? It's a mystery to me." Virginia sighed, high alto. "Tell me, please?"

"I like it here."

"You sound like your father."

"What do you mean?"

"I meant, that's the sort of thing your father would say."

"But do I sound like him?"

"No." Her mother paused. "He would always go off by himself. Antisocial. He'd tell me that he was going away for a couple days and not to ask where, so I never asked. As for who you sound like, if I had to compare you to somebody in the family, you sound like my brother."

"Which is not so bad."

"Why do you say that?"

"Because your baby brother was an interesting person. Uncle John was different from the rest of the family. Nobody ever let him forget it, either. Born twenty years too soon, I think."

"He could have lived at least twenty years longer."

"If what?"

"I didn't say anything." Virginia hummed something religious, like "Rock of Ages" or "Nearer, My God, to Thee." She had poor taste in music, gravitating toward the safe and familiar.

"Did you love him?"

Virginia laughed. "He thought our parents had ruined him. But I'm sure it was the other way around. They certainly cried a lot of tears over Johnny, and they both died young because of him."

"I have to go now."

"Go?"

"I have to get off the phone."

"Your cat misses you."

The cat was hiding under the bed, just her tail showing. "That's right, Mother." Her mother hated to be called Mother.

"What's its name? Ruffles?"

"No. That one died, Mother."

"You're not being very forthcoming with your answers. I'll ask you again. Does your cat have a name?"

"No."

"Is it a boy or a girl?"

"Doesn't matter. Good-bye, Mother."

TENOR

"You still go to that Methodist Church?" he asked his sister, after a long pause in their phone conversation. He was sure that she was crying. He arranged coins on the desktop—six quarters, one nickel.

"Yeah. I can walk to it. Only ten blocks."

"Where's your car?" He panicked, thinking Bob had taken the car from her. Kathy should not be walking around Schenectady—any time of day.

"I'm fine, really. I just like to walk places when I can."

"Do you sing at that church?"

"No. They're too old," she said. "They're as old as Mom and Dad, you know? How old they would be, I meant."

"Late sixties. That doesn't mean they can't sing. We have a couple of people here in their seventies who would amaze you."

"You mean, in your choir?"

"Yeah, my choir. I'll be busy this Christmas." He rubbed two quarters together. "I'm stuck here, if you're trying to lure me to Schenectady."

"I know," she said. "But whenever you return, which you will do, by the way, you could sing with our old choir, actually. They're nice people, very friendly. Not at all intimidating. They'd just love you."

"Maybe."

"And it would be nice," she said, her voice rising in pitch, "if you got a job back in Schenectady. Lawyers can work anywhere."

"You have a lawyer?"

"Of course. But I meant you could get a job here. Certainly, in downtown Albany."

"I like Minneapolis." He picked up a quarter. It seemed to have blue gum permanently stuck to it. A thin wedge of gum came off when he scraped at it. That was old gum. He might have chewed it three years ago, when he had a taste for that color. He was going through a big pack of that gum every day, believing that it kept his voice clear.

"Remember how in the old days when you came home from college and Daddy would have already signed you up for a solo, and you'd get all mad and act like he had signed you up for the Foreign Legion, and you'd say you weren't even going to church that Sunday? And then you would stand up there with the choir and sing in front of everybody, and really knock them out. You just loved it. Your face would turn red and you would act like you were in pain, but you were quite proud of yourself."

"I was never proud."

"Solos would do that to you," she said. "You gloried in them."

"No solos."

"Don't worry. I'll find out when they meet, and you can go if you want. Or stay home. Doesn't matter. It's pretty boring around here otherwise."

"Really? I thought it was rather exciting."

"Divorce only sounds exciting from a distance." She laughed. "There's no drama to this at all."

"Has he been dropping by?"

"No, he has a girlfriend in Clifton Park, who makes good money. A psychiatric nurse, much older. He stays there all the time now."

"A psychiatric nurse," he said, picturing a large woman in a white uniform, grim-faced. "That sounds appropriate."

"At least he has somebody."

"You're lonely."

"No, I was thinking about you. I worry about you." She paused for a second. "You sound tired."

"I'm not."

"You work too much."

To prove he wasn't tired, he sang to her—an old Mendelssohn solo, from *Elijah*. He started soft and grew louder, a slow crescendo, sustaining the phrase on one breath, blasting out the last two words on a triple fortissimo. Before she could comment, he hung up.

Singing loud had stirred up something in his brain. He lay on his side for an hour, slapping his head, poking his little finger in his ear.

If he couldn't kill what was living in there, at least he might stun it, take away its voice. He would choose total silence over this.

BASS

At home, by himself, he sang from the *Methodist Hymnal,* as if getting ready for something. He needed no accompaniment, but would imagine the organ playing under him, offering perfect support, or a professional choir, all the parts done right. He had that skill—of imagining how things should sound. One hardly needed live singers when one had that skill.

SOPRANO

She slept well that night, even with Tara's radio blasting terrible music downstairs well past midnight.

ALTO

She thought of Uncle John, his soft voice—that time he called, five years ago, confused, thinking he had Virginia on the line; soft, almost inaudible, demanding an apology. "I have things to tell you," he had said. "Sit and listen. This will only take five or ten minutes."

"You have the wrong number."

"Please listen."

She had hung up on him, her hand shaking.

TENOR

No dreams. He lay awake all night worrying about the thing in his head, which was dormant now, as if, unlike its host, it had no trouble sleeping. The freeway traffic filled the void.

What was this thing? Cancer? The family had no history of it. His father had always complained of headaches, stomach trouble, claiming he had very little time to live. That was true, but he died of a stroke, and then, it seemed, his mother had dropped dead, from nothing.

BASS

Sunday morning. The choir director at St. Paul's Methodist Church gave him a weird look when she walked by his pew during the recessional. Her head snapped toward him, as if he had done something strange or illegal. He'd been singing. That was all. Singing the melody—belting it out, in the true spirit of the text, where it said, "We'll shout with joy." In this denomination, the congregation was encouraged to sing the hymns, full voice and "lustily," according to John Wesley, whose advice to singers was printed in the front of the hymnal.

Lustily. That word scared him. He closed his mouth, put down the hymnal, and zipped his overcoat, grabbed his hat.

The choir director kept looking at him, her head turned around as if it might become unscrewed. Goofy woman. What did she want? He sneaked out the side door after the benediction.

He stood on the wide steps for a while, kicking at a small patch of ice, diamond-shaped. For a moment he forgot how old he was. He could have been eighteen, fourteen, kicking at the ice on Union Street, the curb in front of the old house, his mother shaking her head in the window. He touched the smooth gray stone where it curved around the doorway, then drew his finger along the mortar. The organ postlude came through the walls of the church, deep, muffled, thunderous; the music resonated in his chest, rising into his head, popping in his ears. It seemed to be insisting on something.

SOPRANO

"The sopranos were just awful," she told Elizabeth at the next voice lesson. These were the first words out of her mouth when she burst into the room, as if she were answering a question that Elizabeth had just asked—as if voice lessons were a continuity in which the rest of the week's activities were nothing more than a brief interruption.

"Who? What were we talking about?"

"My old choir."

"Of course. The tone-deaf ladies." Elizabeth handed her a cup of lemon herb tea. "Listening to untrained voices can cause cell damage in delicate people. Drink this. It will calm you, darling. You need to be calm today."

"I do?"

"You have a disturbing aura," Elizabeth said.

"Sorry."

"That's all right. We'll fix it later. Now talk."

"Okay. I spied on them. I sat in the congregation and listened. Those pitiful sopranos. They were late on every entrance, flat, confused, dragging, never forming a musical phrase. Their heads were bowed, they never opened their mouths. I tell you, Elizabeth, they will be terrible this Christmas. Without me." She sipped from the cup and set it down. The tea was too thick—one part honey to one part water.

"Does that make you happy?"

"What?"

"That they sang so poorly?" Elizabeth pointed to the couch, which was messy. A rumpled green blanket covered the place where she was supposed to lie down. "Stretch out, darling. Take your shoes off. Maybe the shoes are too tight. Bad for the voice."

"I'd just like to forget about that awful choir."

"Wash them out of your brain. All the impurity. There's a wave of pure water flowing through your body right now."

"I wish."

"You still need a place to sing. A home. I'll look into it for you."

"You make it sound like I'm homeless!" She set the teacup on the end table. The tea had not calmed her.

"Which, of course, you're not." Elizabeth smiled slightly. "Not in the least."

She had a nice house, that was true. All the rooms, including the master bath, were larger than this dumpy little studio. "I should have invited you to the house for dinner. The problem is, my husband and daughter and I never sit down and eat a meal together."

"It's hard to schedule things."

"And I can't cook vegetarian." She sipped the last drop of her tea, hoping for an extra jolt of sweetness there.

"You're very busy, darling."

"Christmas will be incredible with all the things Justin and Tara have to do. I'll spend all my time driving Tara from one activity to another, and then Justin will be home from college in a week or two, wanting to borrow my car—you know, his father won't let him use the Mercedes—and I'll be stranded some place downtown. I might be late for choir, if I were still a member." The pillow felt good under her head. It smelled like cinnamon. "I'll hardly miss the choir."

"You will, my darling."

"I will?"

"It's the center of your life."

"My husband is. And my children."

"No, darling, I know you better than that."

"I guess you do."

"I could write your biography."

"Why bother? Nothing has ever happened to me. I'm so depressed without my music." She closed her eyes. "It's like, I would jump out the window if I actually stopped and thought about it."

"Let's not get on that topic again. When you think about bad things, you make it impossible for me to work with you."

"Should I sing now?"

"First let's do breathing exercises, darling."

"Why?"

"It will save your voice. Save you."

"I must be your special project now."

"All my students are special."

"I was afraid you would say that, Elizabeth."

"Why were you afraid I would say that?"

"Because I've heard some of your other students sing, and I fail to see what is special about them."

"I suppose if you're talking about natural talent, then they aren't very special. You're my most talented student, with an absolutely brilliant top."

"Thank you."

"But you don't always sing the best."

"I'm a wreck today."

They did breathing exercises for three minutes, and then the lesson was over. She hadn't sung. And Elizabeth had not fixed her aura.

ALTO

"I have a confession to make," Virginia said on the phone, after asking about the weather.

"Methodists don't make confessions. This must be serious."

"Not really. I mailed you a plane ticket this morning. That's my confession. You'll get it in three or four days."

"Oh, Mother."

"Call me Virginia. I told you I would buy you a ticket a week ago, and you didn't stop me. Don't you miss me?"

"I do."

"We'll pick you up at the Albany Airport. That's convenient for us."

"We? Us?"

"Me. Nothing new to report on that front, sorry to say."

"Uh-huh."

"Just an old reflex," Virginia said.

"Okay, so when does this flight to paradise leave Seattle?"

"On the seventeenth? Is the seventeenth okay?" Bouncy music played in the background, a television show. Either her mother couldn't hear that music or was comforted by it, and so left the TV sound on while talking on the phone.

"I suppose."

"You said you would have your project finished by the fifteenth. That book you were editing?" Virginia must have taken notes on all their phone conversations. "Is everything going okay with the project?"

"Yes, in fact, I just FedExed the final draft."

"FedExed?"

"Mailed it." She inhaled deliberately, as if, while controlling what she said, she had forgotten to breathe during the past few minutes. "All right, you'd better tell me when this plane leaves."

"Eight in the morning. Northwest Airlines. Yes, I'm looking at it now. Terrible handwriting. Let me see what else. And you'll switch planes in Detroit, without any problems, and get in at six, and I'll be there in a red hat, waving at you. How would that work out?"

She paused, considering how to say this. She didn't want to sound ungrateful. "Do you realize how difficult that will be for me?"

"I'm sorry. I'll change it."

"No, I meant that I would have to ride the boat over the day before, and stay with somebody." She thought for a second, then smiled. "I'll stay with Betty. It won't be that much trouble after all."

"Wasn't she in your quartet?"

"No, I used to work with her."

"Another writer."

"Yes, another writer." That was all her mother needed to know.

TENOR

A loud ringing filled his ears. Since he could not drive it away, he studied it. The ringing started on a D and slowly faded to C-sharp, passed from one ear to the other, and vibrated behind his nose, made him want to sneeze, but he couldn't. Was there a worm in his head? A snake? A Gila monster? One night while combing his hair, he felt a bump behind his right ear. When he touched the bump, a chill went down his spine. Worse than a chill: an electric shock.

This might be fatal—if his whole body was wired to it. What would he do with the time he had left? How much longer would he be able to sing decently? A year? Then there would be a slow fadeaway, perhaps, with a memory loss to protect him from great anguish. Good people caring for him, quietly, a softness closing in around him; prayers in a church, perhaps in more than one church, very distant, inaudible; a comforting silence, a soft wrapping up of the senses. In his last days he would forget how he had loved to sing and after he died there would be no record that he had been any good at it.

BASS

On Thanksgiving he helped in the kitchen at St. Paul's, an over-heated room in the church basement, slippery floor, pipes overhead that sweated and dripped. He took off his shirt and peeled potatoes, cut up carrots and celery, spread white frosting with chopped walnuts on three huge spice cakes.

The food smelled wonderful, but he could not eat. He sampled a spoonful of cranberry sauce at the very end of the evening, when the homeless people had gone home, or wherever they had a bed. He let the cranberry sauce slide down very slowly and told his stomach, "Just a bit. You can take it. Give it a chance, buddy. Let it go, nice and easy."

SOPRANO

"I can't take this," she said to herself. They had always dragged her down, the four other regular sopranos at Holy Redeemer Church—Evelyn, Harriet, Brynna, and Maxine. They sang flat. She had tried to pull them up with the force of her voice. Her neck hurt from the effort. Once, in frustration, she had elbowed Maxine in the ribs;

Maxine had fought back, scratching her on the cheek. She still had the scars to show for it.

They had spread their colds, deliberately. Brynna sneezed without covering her mouth, no apologies. Evelyn always had a weird sore on her bottom lip, expanding and contracting, turning colors, never completely fading away, and she never covered her mouth when she coughed, or she touched her lip and then touched other things with the same finger, handed a cookie to somebody with that finger. Those women were all diseased. In the end, they had driven her crazy.

All of this explained why she sang in her throat and how she had ruined her voice whenever she sang with that choir. With all the distractions in the soprano section, she couldn't take proper care of herself. Before each lesson with Elizabeth, she would gargle and warm up on arpeggios, take a long shower, meditate, then vocalize during the fifteen-minute drive to the studio. And then not sing, merely drink tea, do weird exercises, and only talk about singing. And then, to wind down from the lesson, go shopping.

But did anything matter now? She had no choir.

ALTO

That summer she had been walking the west shore road, resting her eyes—late in the evening, still light out, a wide band of ivory in the sky along the northwest islands. Something broke the silence—the outside edges of a string quartet, then the middle strings. This quartet might have played other times when she was walking, but she had missed it because of the headphones or the way the wind blew.

It was real. The musicians stopped and then started again, laughing in between. Real music, a quartet in E major. She squinted through the oak leaves, pulled one branch out of the way, holding her breath. Four people sat on the lawn, two men playing violins, the women playing viola and cello. They wore grungy clothes, or an odd mix of grunge and formal, and they looked so young—early twenties at most. There must have been a music school on the island, or a music camp. She could think of no other explanation. A commune? Brothers and sisters in a family of musicians?

Cousins, perhaps. The men both had long hair—one wore his in a blond ponytail, the other's was dark and loose, sweeping halfway down the back of his tux jacket, swaying as he pulled the bow across the strings, his head tilted in a cocky way, eyes closed. The hair seemed part of the music, as if it had sprung out of it somehow. Both men wore ripped jeans with their tux jackets, and what looked like T-shirts under the jackets. The women wore baggy gray sweatshirts and long black skirts, unlaced combat boots. Their hair was jet black, twisted in tiny buns on their small, intense heads, like ballet dancers—practically twins, although one was Asian, the other European, maybe Hispanic. These kids were so skinny that they might have been ballet dancers.

She looked around, still gripping the branch. Where was the audience for this? What was the purpose? Fun?

She let go of the branch and sat on the stone fence, visible to the musicians, but they were too absorbed to notice her. She was unimportant to their music. They worked with their eyes closed, lacing the strands together, new variations on old themes, then a key change, followed by a stormy fugue that gradually played out into a gentle waltz. She would have stayed much longer, but a dog howled from across the road, so she turned around quickly and went home, a new melody in her head. When she walked through the front door of her cottage, the melody disappeared, absorbed by an indifferent silence, a house full of ordinary objects. The cat snarled at her. The melody would not come back. She tried the piano. The keys resisted, suddenly out of tune. The melody was buried somewhere. She touched the wall, as if the notes were stored in the cold plaster and she could retrieve them that easily. No response. A lampshade throbbed on a dull monotone. In her bathroom, she sat and cried for an hour. "Should I get up and walk back, see if they're still playing?"

TENOR

His favorite hymn tune was "Vineyard Haven," but he could never get them to play it at his church.

BASS

He liked the "Sarum" plainsong chant. And, of course, "Ubi Caritas." Of all the nonchant hymn tunes, he preferred "Forest Green." Vaughan Williams. Anything by Vaughan Williams.

SOPRANO

Her favorite hymn was anything with a high soprano descant.

ALTO

She never went to church. She had no favorite hymn tune.

TENOR

The Three Tenors! Every time he turned on PBS, they were replaying that crap. It was unbearable to watch, even with the mute on—beefy faces, necks straining, eyebrows throbbing. One second of it offended him, just being in the same room while their images crowded the TV screen. Their popularity only proved how bad they were. When he complained about the Three Tenors, his friends thought he was kidding. But he wasn't.

He might have enjoyed the performance if one of the tenors had strangled another or if Pavarotti's gut had exploded. One time he was driving to St. Cloud, dial set on KSJN as usual. He had missed the introduction, so he wondered, Who is this bad tenor, so flat and ordinary? All the passing tones are off pitch. Is this a college performance? Amateur night? When the announcer finally came on and said it had been José Carreras, he was so shocked he nearly hit the median. Then he remembered how Carreras had almost died several years ago—from a brain tumor, or neck cancer. He felt his neck.

BASS

He pulled his belt in another notch. Since last Christmas he had lost forty-five pounds, so he went to the Squire Shop and bought a new wardrobe, featuring a maroon velvet jacket with dark leather buttons, several pairs of gray flannel pants, nice wingtip shoes. He must have looked well turned out, especially his hair—intact, very solid and gleaming. None had fallen out, strong as steel, colored with Just for Men every two or three weeks. Dark brown. He dyed his beard and mustache to match. People were shocked when they found out his age.

He never said, "I'm sixty," but gave out numbers from which sixty could be derived. After a Korean woman sang a program for the church's outreach club, he told her that he knew the words to the Korean national anthem, and then sang it for her right there in the social room as the gathering broke up. One verse. Everybody heard and applauded. Then he sang a folk song.

She asked, "Where did you learn 'Arirang'?"

"I served in Korea. United States Army."

"How long ago were you there?"

"In the war, 1953."

"My goodness, you don't look old enough. I wasn't even born in 1953." She touched his shoulder.

"I was young then."

"A baby."

"Almost." They made a date and he broke it. Or didn't follow up on it, the half-baked promise to see each other.

SOPRANO

Her husband asked why she was still taking voice lessons. She didn't know, but answered, "I have my reasons. Just humor me. The lessons aren't that expensive." If he cut her off, she'd do the same to him, in the most effective way she could. He would regret it, and wonder how he could have been so wrong about her and what she lived for. "It's costing you only twenty a week—to keep me happy."

He was at his desk in the library, going through the canceled checks for the month. "I'm not complaining about the cost."

"It's a lifeline."

"You don't have to convince me with fancy words, whatever that crazy teacher hands you." He twirled his finger next to his ear. "I only asked about it because you're not singing anywhere. That I know of."

"Give me a month or two."

"No deadlines." He sharpened his pencil. "I wouldn't force any deadlines on you. I just wanted to know."

ALTO

She dreamed that the barbershop quartet had reunited and settled their disputes. In the dream, they were singing in the dark, near open water. She could hear all the parts more clearly than ever, and she blended easily, without pain. Why couldn't it ever be perfect like that when she was awake? Her quartet had always gone flat, from pushing too hard, not listening to each other. She had perfect pitch, and it physically hurt when they went flat, so much that she would double over, run out of the room, and shake her head until the bad notes dissolved in static. The other three women had thought she was crazy.

Maybe if they had all lived together in a commune, cooked for each other, thrown all their income into a single pot. If they had sat out on a lawn, late into the evening, and made music with a real passion, eyes closed, hair flying. If they had lived that way, they could have stayed on pitch and kept the group together, and she would not be so depressed.

TENOR

The Three Tenors—more like a geological formation than a musical ideal. They blocked the light, cast a shadow upon the soul.

He believed that the ideal tenor voice was focused and pure, no vibrato—or just a slight touch of it, sufficient to keep the musical line going. The ideal tenor should sound like a strong alto, and if an alto and tenor were singing the same note, mezzo piano, they should be indistinguishable, as if they were one person.

Often he sang while driving to work, testing the vowels on every note of his two-octave range. If he sang at home, the upstairs neighbors pounded on the floor with a broom handle and took revenge late at night, laughing, mocking his voice, singing like a fat opera star. So, at home, he sang within himself and, while he sang, managed to drive away the terrible ringing, the snake that had eaten into his brain. Thus far, it had spared his throat, although certain mornings when he awoke, he felt a vague thing tickling in there, reaching into the part of himself that he valued most and hoped to protect the longest. He gargled for five minutes and swallowed three vitamin C pills, garlic, and ginger tablets. He limited the amount of speaking he did at work, said hi to each co-worker only once per day.

BASS

Arirang, arirang, a-ra-i-o. Arirang co-gae-ro nomo-kanda. The old words came back. If there was a second verse, he had never learned it.

Korea, 1953. North of Seoul. A young woman in an abandoned church had taught him that single verse while he sat on a primitive bench, smiling at her. Taught it to him one line at a time. The music was the only verbal connection between them—a haunting melody. They could not understand each other. He only knew how to say hello and good-bye. She only knew how to say "Number ten" and "Number one."

They sang "Arirang" once more, a unison duet, holding hands, iron tight, almost hurting each other.

And now his hands shook for a moment, so strong was the memory.

He felt his hair, solid, pulled at it, and none came out. None of the hair dye showed on his fingertips.

He was only seventeen but he should have married her and brought her back to the States. She was a fine soprano, at least in his memory, her voice warm and inviting. She could have learned English and sung with him for the past forty years as he moved from choir to choir. If he could have kept her that long.

SOPRANO

Along the inside wall of the family room she had established a musical shrine, a montage of souvenir programs and photos, the highlights of a third-rate singing career—talent shows, operas, college choir, church choir, a recital or two. As she squinted at the old photos, thinking about the people who had sung with her, unable to remember any faces to go with the names, her husband came up behind her and said, "We never finished that conversation. I asked you why you weren't singing in a choir."

"I told you, I'm on hiatus."

"Are you unhappy?"

"Not really," she said. "It's so busy right now I have hardly any time to think about whether I'm unhappy."

"But you once told me you were happiest when singing."

"I guess I was," she said.

He walked away, the ice clinking in his glass. Well, it was true! Her husband couldn't make her happy; he could only make her comfortable, tolerate her, keep her off the streets—where she might walk like a crazy woman, singing with wild abandon, like Elizabeth, who was almost homeless.

The top left photo was a close-up of the old folk trio, which had gotten together during her first semester in college. She was chubby then, her cheeks just huge, as if she had stored food in them. One forgettable guy with big eyes and one other girl, with a name something like Mary Ann, who was incredibly beautiful, long blond hair and huge eyes, and looked as if she could sing like an angel. Mary Ann sang like a devil, always wandering off onto another pitch and forgetting the lyrics, as if she had focused too much on her looks.

One night they had performed together in a coffeehouse just off campus, in the basement of a used bookstore, a place with an odd name. The Penultimate? They sang early sixties folk standards. A woman, a dark little woman with short dark hair and large hoop earrings—this woman had come up to her and said, "You're wasted in that group," as if she were an expert.

After that remark, the soprano had taken voice theory and sung in the college chapel choir, where she was given an occasional solo. She had tried out for musicals and had not looked right for any of the leads. They had told her they were glad to have her singing in the chorus, usually as a peasant. She was in the chorus of *Brigadoon* for a month of rehearsals, then quit. Too much dancing. Her feet hurt and her voice wasn't getting much of a workout.

Brigadoon? She had just seen something about that show, something that annoyed her. Her husband walked by and snapped his fingers in her face.

"I'm not in a trance."

Tara walked by and did the same thing. The whole family must have thought she was crazy.

ALTO

The alto walked slowly to the shore. She might have been in a dream. She dropped to her knees and leaned over the water. It was mirror calm, but did not give back a clear reflection. The wind stirred up a slight ripple, and now her head looked like a monster, peering through distorted venetian blinds. "Who are you? What is your name?"

She felt her neck and chin. They seemed shapeless, fat. She needed to jog an extra two miles every day.

TENOR

One time he had been hanging out with Kathy and Bob in New York City, midtown. He could not remember the exact occasion, or even the year. He had been about to take the bar exam. Probably 1980. Kathy was living in New York then, or still in school, Fashion Institute of Technology. Bob worked part-time as a messenger boy, in good shape back then, from riding around the city on a bicycle, wearing a backpack.

The three of them had stopped at a game arcade in midtown and cut a record. It was some kind of coin-operated contraption, in a soundproof booth, where they paid four quarters to cut a one-minute record—a disc, with the audio quality of an old Edison cylinder. He still had it among his things. Bob must have been standing closest to the mike, since his voice blocked out the other two. The damn fool was chanting "Booga, booga, booga" endlessly.

"Bob can't sing," he had whispered to Kathy, outside. "Not one note."

"So what?" she had asked. "We can't all be perfect like you."

"I wasn't implying that."

"Singing isn't everything."

Later, however, the fact that Bob could not sing became important to Kathy. It became a character flaw, the first of many.

BASS

The choir director wrote him in November: "So, my dear sir, I was at Miss Kim's talk and heard your glorious baritone voice." The loopy words were squeezed on the back of an oversize Beethoven postcard that had taken three days to arrive, although mailed in the same city. "Please tell me this—what can I do to get you to join the choir? It's a sin for you not to be singing in a choir. I really mean that. You, who physically resemble Robert Goulet, and sing even more beautifully. Singing is everything. Sincerely, Donna."

When he flipped the card and looked at Beethoven, in black and white, the huge brooding forehead and deep eyes, he imagined what Donna sounded like, her speaking voice. A battle-ax.

He wrote back: "Perhaps I'll join you for Christmas. No long-term commitment, though. I'm retired, and so, from time to time, especially in cold weather, I would be taking off on vacation. Perhaps to

Camelot!" She called two days later and spoke so sweetly to him, he wondered just what he had agreed to.

SOPRANO

"Elizabeth! I'm depressed. Do you have any pills? Any special herbs that could cure my depression?" She stepped toward Elizabeth's tiny kitchen, through another set of beaded curtains, beige and white, that slapped against the back of her legs. There were no doors in the studio, a fact that had something to do with the psychology of singing.

"Nothing in there for you today. Sorry."

"Then what will help me?" It was cold in the studio. She kept her coat on and sat down. The couch needed new springs. At the very least, it needed to be tuned.

"Just music, darling."

"It won't work. My God, this couch is awful."

"Yes it will," Elizabeth said. "Oh, I almost forgot to tell you, I have something for you. My best friend, Donna Rodman, called me. Did I ever mention Donna?"

"No." She had thought that *she* was Elizabeth's best friend. In fact, Elizabeth had told her that three times.

"Smile, darling. Like this." She drew a little curve in front of her mouth. "This is wonderful news. Donna says she's looking for a trained soprano to help out with her special music this Christmas." She nodded rapidly.

"Do I have to drive a hundred miles?"

"No, darling, it's right here in Schenectady. Isn't that wonderful! five miles from your house."

"What kind of music do they sing? Evangelical? Spirituals?"

"Good music."

"What would they pay?"

"Twenty a week!" Elizabeth seemed amazed by that figure, as if a person could live in splendid luxury on twenty a week. "That would break down to ten dollars for the rehearsal, ten more for the service. You would also get the weddings and funerals, which are worth much more, as you know, because you're not dealing with the church treasurer, but with families. Families can be quite generous. I once got two hundred for a wedding, and all I did was sing a five-minute love song.

I didn't have to stay and socialize—"

"I'll think about it. When would I start?"

"Right away."

"I'd really have to think about joining a new choir. It's such a major decision. Like getting married."

"Do it."

"I'll go listen to them, and then make up my mind. They don't have to know right away."

"Grab it while you can, darling."

"Why? Because I'm getting old?"

"No. I'm only saying that the world of music will never reach out and embrace you. If anything, it will reach out and slap you in the face."

She stared at Elizabeth, whose thin cheeks were bright red. Slapped. "All right," she said. "I'll sit in on a rehearsal or two. Hide in the dark. Go to church a couple of Sundays and see what I think. Wear a veil." She covered her face and said nothing for a minute. "Maybe I should become a nun."

"What?"

"In a nice little convent, singing every day. That would make me happy. I don't want to say yes to this church and then be stuck in an unpleasant situation. Trapped, having to smile all the time and be nice to people."

"What do you expect? What would make you happy, darling?"

"Perfection."

ALTO

Nothing would make her happy. Nothing. Certainly not seeing her mother again, staying two weeks in that awful house where she couldn't control anything. The only thing that could make her happy would be to pick up where she had left off—a couple of significant places in her past. Twenty years ago. Two years ago. A month ago, on an evening walk.

TENOR

Good health, a reprieve from chronic pain. Respect from his colleagues. A wider seat on this airplane, nobody sitting in the middle seat. No babies screaming. Many small things could make him happy.

On airplane flights he could ask himself questions and work out reasonable answers.

To discover that this noise in his head was nothing more than the sound of an engine. To step off the plane and have that noise disappear.

Or how about this? To perform a piece of music perfectly, using that ideal tenor voice he had been cultivating.

BASS

To be twenty again, for a year, would make him very happy. Not to be twenty in 1956, which had been a bad year for him, romantically, but to be twenty right now, and see how he fared, musically, socially. Of course, he'd have plenty of money and wouldn't have to look for a job.

To be twenty for a year.

A year could be spaced out into vast stretches of good time. If one took each day at the proper pace and lived fully in the moment, then a year could feel like a lifetime—of which it was the epitome—and if one lived just one good year and then died on the last day, so be it.

SOPRANO

"No," she said to Elizabeth. "Perfection wouldn't do it. I'd like to revise my answer. Ask me again."

"What would make you happy, darling?"

"Sincere praise. For my singing."

"You're wonderful," Elizabeth said, without a pause. "How's that?"

"I haven't even sung yet today. And last week I didn't sing at all."

"I was just remembering all the wonderful times in the past. Your work on the Bach *Magnificat* a year ago. Wonderful."

"But, Elizabeth," she said, "I want sincere praise for the way I sing now."

"All right. Sing!"

Still lying on the couch, she opened her mouth and started to sing: "Laudate Domine . . ."

"Get up! You can't sing from there! My God, haven't you learned anything from me?"

"Maybe I haven't."

"I have taught you posture. I've taught you that much, I hope."

"Sorry." She stood up and sang a quick arpeggio, rippling from middle C up to the very top of her range, and then down again. She waited until her head cleared before asking Elizabeth, "Well?"

"Wonderful!"

"Really?"

"It rang in the walls, darling. It came right out of the mask and shook the entire house."

"I hope I didn't break anything!"

"It would be worth it." Elizabeth looked around, as if checking for damage. "You're making progress. As I've said many times, you have it in you—a perfect voice. In fact, everybody does."

"Everybody? That's depressing."

ALTO

Under all that crap lay buried a perfect voice. She gargled three times a day, alternating between Chloraseptic and blue mint Listerine, spitting in the sink, then rinsing with spring water. She sang using her head voice, wanted to sound like a violin, moving gently up the scale, past middle C, toward a place where she believed her voice would be most comfortable. If she stayed light, the voice was fine, smooth. If she pushed, her throat became scratchy. It was as if she were on the edge of retrieving a beautiful object she had lost. Something she had thrown away, in fact.

TENOR

"Would you like to go to choir rehearsal tonight?" Kathy squeezed his shoulder as he set down the duffel and backpack in Bob's old room, next to an unplugged and somewhat dented jukebox.

Out of breath, slightly dizzy, he pressed his hand against the wall so he wouldn't collapse. "Just a minute." Part of him hoped that Kathy was dating, that some guy would be coming over that evening. Another part thought, She can't protect herself. "You want to be alone in the house for a couple hours, is that it?"

"No, I intended to go with you. The thing is, I promised the choir you would show up tonight."

"What?"

"Sorry. They're desperate for tenors."

"Yeah," he said. "They'd have to be desperate to want me."

She frowned, then petted him on the shoulder. "I shouldn't have said that. They're really nice people. And even if they were desperate, they would be thrilled to have even the best tenor in the world show up at rehearsal. Like Pavarotti?"

"In that case, they would be desperate."

"That's right, you hate him."

"Let's just say that you wouldn't want Pavarotti in a church choir. He'd never blend. He'd misbehave, start dating the organist." He sat on the bed. The room was spinning slightly, tipping away from him. "I'll go, but no solos. Okay?"

"I won't volunteer you for anything." She touched his knee. "Are you hiding something from me, Luciano? Are you feeling all right?"

"Yeah, I'm fine."

"We could go skiing this weekend." She clapped her hands. "Gore Mountain? What do you think?"

"No thanks."

"Put a little color in your cheeks. You look a bit grayish."

"Comes from working under fluorescent lights."

"I'd never heard about that."

"It's a joke. Fluorescent lights won't do that to you." He doubted anything would put color in his cheeks.

BASS

He arrived at rehearsal five minutes early. As soon as he walked into the practice room, the choir director kissed him on the cheek. Donna. They were the same height, so he didn't have to bend at all to return the kiss. She hugged him, too, and he let his arms hang loose while that happened.

"Whoa," he finally said when the hug got too intense, a bone-crusher. "Let's just take it easy there, lady."

"Have a doughnut." Donna let go of him and pointed to a side table, which was loaded with several boxes of doughnuts, in various shapes and colors. Blue icing, pink icing, sprinkles, and coconut. Chocolate frosting. The coffeepot bubbled. Good coffee. He could smell it.

"Sorry," he said. "I can't eat doughnuts and then sing. After rehearsal, maybe I'll take a plain brown doughnut."

"Have a cup of coffee."

"Can't do that either."

"All negatives." She frowned. "Let me try another question, and don't say no until you hear it."

"Sorry," he said, laughing. "Can't do it."

She picked up her white baton and pointed it at his chest. "In a week, my dear, we'll be doing some special music, for the season."

"Uh-huh."

"How about singing a little solo for me?" She waved the baton a few times, as if conducting him.

"Take it easy," he laughed, raising his hands to protect his face from the baton. "I don't read music very well. The eyes aren't what they used to be, ha-ha. The voice either."

"Don't hand me that."

"Really," he said. "I'm old. I have my good days, but mostly bad days. A lot of out-of-tune, tight-in-the-throat days."

"Sure, uh-huh. Come on, eat one little doughnut. You need a sugar boost, honey." She held a powdered doughnut to his lips and he took one small bite, held it in his cheek. When Donna turned to greet another singer, he spit the chewed doughnut into a napkin and tossed it in the wastebasket.

SOPRANO

They were too old! Older than she was! Sixties, seventies. Eighties! Would it be worth it for this church to pay the twenty a week? What difference could one professional soprano make in such an ancient and decrepit choir? But she had come to church service again the following Sunday and figured she would sit up front with the choir pretty soon. Make a few friends. At least take the opportunity to test the vocal cords. She had not sung in public for a month. She could show off at rehearsal, bask in their praise.

It was as if something had been missing from her blood the past few weeks. Or by not singing that long, she had given up a form of protection that singing provided, an immunity against hopelessness.

ALTO

Her second day back in Schenectady, she lay on the living room couch reading a year's worth of *National Geographics,* tossing them in a messy pile as she finished them. The pictures weren't as pretty as they used to be. Virginia came in, clapped her hands, and asked, "Are you asleep?"

"No, just reading about pollution in Eastern Europe."

"Your eyes have been closed for more than an hour."

"I'm not sleeping, Mother."

"I have a favor to ask." She leaned close, as if to whisper in her ear. "Not a big favor."

She squinted at her mother. "Okay. I'll call you Virginia."

"That's not it. I can't see to drive very well, especially when it's dark out. Would you drive me to choir tonight, my dear?"

She closed the magazine and sat up. "Really?"

"My night vision is going."

"What?"

"Don't panic. It's not all that serious. Over the past couple of years, my eyesight has been fading."

"What else don't I know about your health?"

"A touch of arthritis in my hands." Virginia held her right hand in front of the lamp. The light shone through, in shades of amber.

"All right," she said. "I'll drive you to choir. It's not a stick shift, is it?"

"Of course not."

"If it was, I was gonna say that you could drive and I could sit on the passenger side and keep you on the road by shouting directions at you." She laughed. "But my voice is a wreck. I can't shout. I can't sing."

"You can sit and listen. I wouldn't make you sing."

"Hah!"

"I've learned my lesson," Virginia said, with a vague smile. "A long time ago. The Christmas pageant, when they were looking for an angel and I volunteered my beautiful daughter, who somehow disappeared into a closet. Anyway, they have their own soloists."

"I never sing solos."

"Too bad."

TENOR

The old man in the next chair cleared his throat, put a handkerchief to his mouth, wiped his lips, then angled his head slightly toward him. The choir hadn't sung anything yet. "How're ya doing tonight, young fella?"

"Fine."

"I wanted to tell ya, in case you haven't heard, the Christmas party is at my place this year. Here's a map of how to get there. Blue house, white shutters."

The photocopied map was spotted with coffee stains. Arrows went left and right and up and down, and a huge X marked the spot. The handwriting was terrible. He couldn't make out any of the street names. "Thanks. I don't know."

"You're new in the choir. I wanted you to feel at home with us."

"That's nice."

"Day after New Year's. You don't have to bring anything to the party. A bottle of booze if you want."

He smiled at the old man. "I'm afraid I have to be back in Minneapolis by New Year's."

"Don't give me that."

"I'm just visiting."

"They all say that."

The choir sat and waited. Their director seemed completely disorganized, huddling with various small groups, chattering and laughing. The tenor couldn't hear a word of it, because the internal ringing had started up again. He slapped the side of his head, gently.

BASS

Donna kept looking at him, mouthing a word that had a long *o* in it. Was she trying to get him to change his mind about the solo? No solos. He planned to keep a low profile during his first season with the choir, wait until next year, see how the stomach felt. He fished a lemon mint Maalox tablet from his pocket and chewed on it slowly. By next year he might be wearing a bag, or adult-size disposable diapers.

He mouthed back at Donna, "No solo." She smiled, misreading his lips.

The sopranos practiced a descant and seemed much improved. When had they suddenly learned to sing on pitch?

SOPRANO

At least these people smile at me, she thought. Unlike those crabby old bitches at Holy Redeemer. Do they like my voice, is that it?

She touched her cheek, where the scar, three parallel lines, raked diagonally toward her mouth.

No more fighting.

ALTO

They arrived late, had to park on the street and step through snow-banks and wipe their shoes on the welcome mat. Why did her mother still attend this old church, a half-hour drive from home? Virginia had kept telling her, "You could drive faster," but the roads were icy and the lighting was poor. The car kept sliding.

The church smelled like mothballs and rancid sweat. She started to take off her sweatshirt, but all she wore under it was a tank top. That wouldn't go over very well.

Virginia picked up a copy of *The Upper Room,* then led the way downstairs to a door that said Choir Practice on a gray cardboard sign. The room was stuffy—twenty people in wool clothing and bad per-fume, all whispering, while a broad-shouldered woman with bouffant gray-blond hair played piano.

The woman stopped playing the piano, looked at them, and said, "Hello, Virginia. And who is this?"

"My long-lost daughter."

"Soprano or alto?"

She answered for herself, "Doesn't matter."

"How about tenor? We're short on tenors."

"I'll try the alto. Okay?"

Her mother smiled. They sat next to each other and shared music. Virginia barely sang, produced no audible sound. Choir rehearsal must have been a social occasion, to fill a great emptiness in her life. One time her mother had called, and the real issues came to the sur-face. Virginia had started criticizing her for living the way she did. "You need a husband, or at least a boyfriend." She had answered back, "And you need a hobby, Virginia. A new hobby, one that has nothing to do with me and telling me what I need all the time." When she was upset, she used her mother's name, pronounced it like a dirty word, with a snarl on the third syllable. She moved her lips, cursing under her breath; Virginia patted her arm.

A quartet was being talked about, with great anxiety. The music was just "Lo, How a Rose E'er Blooming." No big deal, but three of the four singers who had been scheduled to sing the quartet evidently were missing or incapacitated. A very tall man with thick glasses and abundant white hair started waving at the choir director, gesticulating in some primitive sign language. Finally, he drew his finger across his throat, as if to say, "The voice is gone."

"Lord help me," the choir director wailed, with hands supplicating heavenward. "Now we need replacements for everybody! It's a disaster!"

The alto closed her eyes. These people were pathetic. What a waste of time. When would the choir finally get around to singing? The rehearsal would be over in less than an hour. Perhaps the evening would break up into complete anarchy, or its musical equivalent.

She had humored Virginia, driven her to rehearsal, kept her company. Now she was losing her inner balance. She meditated about the island, the sound of waves, and other things that flowed, seamlessly. The discussion continued, three thousand miles away from the place to which she had traveled while meditating, the words so plain and ugly. These people had the worst speaking voices.

Tenor

Three in the section, besides him, all men. Tenors always looked half-baked, drained of all energy, yellow-eyed, guilty of a secret crime.

Bass

Basses were usually lazy tenors. He would not include himself in that category, since he had never sung tenor. He always thought that tenors were incomplete in some fundamental way, smiled too much, went bald at a young age, fought among themselves, talked funny. What was that book title? *Men, Women, and Tenors.* Basses were normal men.

Soprano

Sopranos, with certain exceptions (and Elizabeth was definitely not among the exceptions), should be institutionalized, taken out only for rehearsals and Sunday service, properly medicated.

Alto

She looked at them—the average alto was seventy-five years old and always a widow. Seven altos in a row, all the same, smiling for some reason.

Tenor

The choir director clicked her baton four times against the top rim of her music stand. "Luckily, we have a replacement for Kimberly on the soprano part," she announced in a very loud voice. "And it's not me." Everybody laughed. "You all know how I sing. I couldn't blend with a milkshake. But this beautiful young lady will be terrific. She's just joined the choir." Using the baton, she pointed toward a thin woman with curly red hair, hardly young, hardly beautiful, who seemed outraged and flattered at the same time—if that was possible.

"And this dear gentleman sitting here in the bass section," she continued, grabbing the shoulder of a good-looking man in a maroon jacket, possibly wearing a toupee, "who has been hiding out in the congregation much too long—"

"Only two months," he interrupted, softly, too high to be a true bass.

"—much, much too long, and who has now joined us, at least for the season. This lovely gentleman will be a fine replacement for poor Harold, whose laryngitis, I assure you, is genuine, although I was thinking of asking for a doctor's note."

The choir laughed and applauded.

"But the tenor and alto are still a problem. I really don't know how we'll cover the inner voices. Whoever you are—the perfect mates for the lovely soprano and bass who have already volunteered—I know you'll feel it in your hearts before we finish tonight. Perhaps God will tell you what to do. Don't be modest." She closed her eyes and tipped her head toward the ceiling. "I can tell that you're both in this room. I can feel it."

He shook slightly. Of course, he was the one, the "perfect tenor," but this felt like manipulation. Kathy gave him a look, from where she sat along the rear wall—raised her head slightly and pursed her lips.

He closed his eyes. He had held back this time, kept the voice soft and anonymous. The fact was, he could have blasted the whole choir off the map, if the situation required, and there had been such situations. Choir directors in various churches had told him to cool it, even when the music called for maximum volume from all parts. And then he would really cool it, turn down the volume to pianissimo, so they'd have to relent and say, "Not *that* soft, please. We need to hear you." And he would smile, thinking how people needed to hear him.

There were important people in his church back in Minneapolis— rich executives, college presidents, political figures. Crime figures. He liked to think that such people had heard him sing, had given him their full attention.

"Oh, all right," a woman finally said, and stood up. She had very short blond hair, no makeup, and concealed whatever figure she had beneath a bulky sweatshirt and khaki pants. An older woman sitting nearby clapped loudly.

"Alto?" the choir director asked.

"Well, my mother showed me the part, and it lies within my range. I could handle it okay. This is for—what? Christmas Eve?"

"Christmas morning."

"How early? I'm suffering from jet lag."

"Eleven o'clock service."

"All right, I'll do it. My juices should be flowing by then. My mother can pump me full of coffee. I'll probably sound like a water buffalo."

"You'll be just fine. Now," the choir director said, clapping vigorously, "would someone please lend me a tenor?"

The old tenor gave him a nudge, but he shook his head, very slightly. For the first time in a month, he had tamed the beast that had invaded his brain. He did not want to enrage it again.

BASS

Without a tenor, the quartet would not happen. The bass smiled as he browsed through the hymnal, checking the index for odd tune names. It didn't matter to him one way or the other. He wanted to chant something, not sing four-part harmony, which always felt cluttered, messy. Chanting was clean, unified, thrilling. He still missed it, although not so much that he would run off and join a monastery.

The choir took a break. A thin young man in wire-rim glasses, slightly balding, lingered near the doughnuts, talking with a blond girl whom the bass had seen waiting in the back of the room. They talked very softly.

Donna gave the young man a poke. "You take one more doughnut from that table and you'll owe me something!"

"Sorry. I'm a sugarholic."

"Bad for the voice," she said. "Very bad." She pretended to slap his wrist.

"*You* ate a couple."

"Hey, I don't have to sing. I never follow my own rules. Why should I? All I ever do is wave my arms around like this, hoping people will watch." She demonstrated, in three-four time. Donna was too physical. "I need the sugar to keep my body going."

"I have sort of a headache. Tired, I guess."

"You're a good singer."

"How could you possibly know?" He scratched behind his ear and winced. "I haven't made any noise tonight."

"I can tell by looking," she said.

"Looking good isn't enough."

"I didn't say you were handsome." She bit into a powdered doughnut, which spurted red jelly onto her chin. It ran down her neck, and further, probably streaking her breast. "I'm talking about posture, head shape, jaw position. Your eyes. There's a certain look in the eyes that tells the world, 'I can sing.' And you have it." She shook the doughnut at him.

"You want me for the quartet?"

"Yes. I know how good you are. Why resist?"

"All right."

"You're a doll." She wiped her fingers on a napkin, then gave his hand a squeeze. "Come early next time. Fifteen minutes early. I'll have the quartet go over the piece while the others are spilling their coffee. Once or twice will be enough. It's very easy. Can you sight-read?"

"I do it all the time."

"Good. I knew it. You know, we have money in this church to pay soloists. I might sign you up as our regular tenor soloist. I could go as high as fifty dollars a week—for a tenor. Sixty! And I could get you extra work, at a nice fee. There's a synagogue in town that pays well. How about it?"

"Just visiting. I have a real job somewhere else."

"Uh-huh," she said. "Sure."

Donna would scare him away if she kept pressing. The poor fellow shook, as if in terror. The young woman walked over to him and massaged his arm, and then they got their coats and left.

SOPRANO

She dreamed that Elizabeth had broken into her bedroom and sucked all the breath out of her.

ALTO

She dreamed that Virginia had gone blind and asked her to move in permanently. "I'll pay you. I'll give you all my money. And you can work on your writing here, just as well as you ever could on that island of yours."

She dreamed that this would be the rest of her life, what she would do until she was very old. The best thing in her life would be this choir. Her mother would live to 104, like Rose Kennedy.

TENOR

He dreamed of the noise that lived inside him. A buzzing noise. He dreamed that the snakes had taken over his entire brain. There was no space left for singing, even the memory of singing.

BASS

He never dreamed. Almost never. He did recall a dream from at least a month ago in which his old choir director (the one who had been fired) had seated him and three other people in a row, in an empty cell-like room, trying to teach them a new chant. The problem was, the words were nonsense, pig latin, and the notes followed an ugly sequence, like Schoenberg.

QUARTET

On the Sunday morning when the quartet would be performed, the choir walked through unshoveled snow and rubbed their shoes against the stiff brushes that were mounted just outside the church door. They barked the usual greetings. Everybody came early, the whole choir—obsessive early birds, flying about with their robes half open, grabbing their music and church programs, vocalizing in the limited ways they knew. Knee, neigh, gnaw. These other sopranos, altos, tenors, and basses stood on the opposite side of the room, across from the quartet. They had been talking, munching on iced red and green sugar cookies, but as soon as Donna played a harsh chord on the piano, they set down their cookies, dumped the coffee into the sink, and listened carefully, as the quartet sang together for the first time.

The choir hoped to learn from watching them—how they stood in a tight circle, leaned into the middle, made eye contact with each other. Good singing was a mystery. The four seemed to probe each other in a subtle way, squinting, smiling, tipping their heads.

They might be another species of animal, so different were they from the other singers.

They breathed together and sang, in the key of E major:

Lo, how a Rose e'er blooming . . .

Each syllable was perfectly blended. It would be hard to pull the voices apart, to analyze who was singing what, although the alto and tenor moved separately in certain measures. Something about the walls and ceiling smoothed out any edges, the borders between voices, the measure lines that would be visible on the page of music. The choir members followed along silently, moving their lips. This was the limit of their ability. They could not imitate what happened inside a trained singer, whatever the human body did when it sang correctly.

Donna had described it for them once—the soft palate, the diaphragm, the way they should position their tongues, resonate in the sinuses, and so on. She had drawn pictures on the blackboard, with detailed cutaways of the mouth, throat, and nasal cavities. She had even hugged them, as if to squeeze out the proper sound or reshape their bodies. "Anybody can sing!" "Not us!" they replied. "Oh yes you can," she said, and hugged them again, but this was during her first year with the choir, and she had calmed down considerably in recent years.

And now everybody watched Donna, for her reaction to the music, for a verification of what was happening in that room. They looked at her hands. She seemed to be holding an invisible ball, about the size of a cantaloupe, slowly turning it, examining the surface for dents or bruises, finding none.

The quartet stopped for a few seconds, laughed about something, evidently a mistake, then started again. No part was any louder than the other three. A dozen people might have been singing. Or a single voice that could clone itself, divide in four.

From tender stem hath sprung.

An hour later, during the offertory, when the four strangers stood up and sang the quartet in public, the notes sounded as if they had come out of the organ, with consonants attached, as if a strong wind had blown through the wall from outside and swept through the pipes, all at once. It was that strong and, at times, a bit cold, not warmed to room temperature.

Finally, it warmed, and the harmony spread out like soft gold paint, covering every surface, evenly. Complete contact.

Of Jesse's lineage coming . . .

Programs rattled under the four voices, as the congregation checked to see who was who, but all it said was "Special Music." The singers remained anonymous robed figures. Maybe the preacher would make a special mention of them during the announcements.

As men of old have sung.
It came, a floweret bright,
Amid the cold of winter,
When half spent was the night.

Some fool clapped, twice loudly, then once faintly, but there was one more verse, which flowed more smoothly, the voices now finely adjusted to each other. No mistakes, not even the thought of a mistake—if one read their faces correctly. Not one vowel wrongly shaded, not one pitch off by the slightest deviation, not one attack too light, too strong, too early, or too late. No physical distractions, no nervous shaking, swaying, foot-tapping. Solid and professional.

The congregation raised their heads, as if there might be some huge rose window to meditate on, or sculptured tracery, softened by a haze of incense.

A plain white ceiling was all they had. It was enough.

> *Isaiah 'twas foretold it,*
> *The Rose I have in mind.*
> *With Mary we behold it,*
> *The Virgin Mother kind.*
> *To show God's love aright,*
> *She bore to us a Saviour,*
> *When half spent was the night.*

They ended on a slight ritard, clipping the final consonant in absolute unison, plucking it like an icicle from the edge of a roof. Something hung in the air, a light glaze of purity, and a hope for another verse. Fearful of breaking such a fragile thing, nobody moved. Ten seconds. Then the quartet folded back into the choir, their faces in shadow. Someone in the choir dropped a hymnal, laughed nervously. A door slammed. Several people coughed violently. The preacher did not thank the quartet. He began to pray for the sick and the dead, and the congregation recognized the names, made mental notes to call or visit. But nobody heard the sermon. Nobody heard the prayers, or the benediction.

SOPRANO

"My husband is home watching the children," she said to several sweet ladies who approached her in the narthex and chirped about how well she had sung.

Now why did I say that to them? she immediately thought. My children hardly need watching. I should have thanked these ladies. They'll think I'm a terrible snob.

"You were wonderful!"

That was a plural "you," referring to the quartet. She could not have sung a wonderful solo. The other three parts had carried her, made her sound like a pro. The four of them would sing together again, but not every week. Perhaps they could meet at each other's homes, work on new music, branch out and sing folk music, madrigals. She was curious to see how the other three lived. Did they have nice pianos? The bass, who looked rich, might even have a harpsichord.

"Really wonderful. I mean it."

"Thank you." She felt almost giddy. But she never believed the praise of amateurs. She needed to hear from Elizabeth.

ALTO

For several minutes she cried in the ladies' room. She did not know why she was so miserable.

When she stopped to catch her breath, she heard another woman crying in the next stall. It wasn't the soprano from the quartet—who had seemed so vulnerable, ready to burst into tears at any moment—but a deep voice, like hers. What could bring on such grief?

Maybe the sense that she had settled for mediocrity, that she had made too many excuses for not doing things all her life.

TENOR

"What is that thing behind your ear?" Kathy asked, as they walked to the parking lot. "It's bleeding behind your ear."

"Mosquito bite."

"That's no mosquito bite. On Christmas? In upstate New York? You'd better tell me. What is it?"

"Nothing."

"You need someone to take care of you," she said, running to catch up with him. "Don't you have a friend to take care of you?"

"Leave me alone." The music had set that damn snake loose again.

"When was the last time you went to a doctor?"

"1980."

BASS

In the church office, Donna kissed him, hard, on the lips. An hour ago, near the end of the quartet, he had been short of breath, and could have benefited from mouth-to-mouth resuscitation. But at this particular moment, no sir. He was fine. Donna held on tight—one damn strong woman. They rolled off the small couch onto the linoleum floor, among extra programs and pledge cards.

Now she was sucking all the air out of him. He pushed her away and stood up.

"What's wrong?"

"The church office? Right after service? It's too risky."

"I locked the door," she said.

The door had a map of the county, with various colored pins stuck into it. "I need to get home and eat dinner."

"That's a lame excuse if I ever heard one."

SOPRANO

Well, my darling, she said to herself while driving, your husband is home watching the children, or a football game, and he could have been here, listening to you. What you just gave those people was worth at least fifty dollars.

They have no idea of the value. A hundred dollars would be a bargain. Who knows? A thousand!

ALTO

"Where were you?" Virginia asked. "I've been waiting twenty minutes."

"Five minutes. I'm fine."

"I didn't ask you that."

"I'm fine."

"All right, then tell me this. What are you going to do next?"

"Drive home with you and get a few hours of sleep. I'm totally wiped out. From stress." She took a deep breath. She wanted a cigarette, a drug to put her out. It wasn't the singing that had stunned her. Couldn't have been. The singing was the easy part of this deal.

"What about the social hour? I wanted to introduce you to my friends."

"Let's skip it," she said. "I'd rather lie down and sleep the rest of the day. I still have jet lag." She held the outside door for Virginia, then tried to steer her toward the car.

"What will you do after that?"

"Tomorrow?"

"I mean, in the coming weeks, what will you do for an encore? You and your three new friends."

"I don't even know their names, Mother!"

"I'll get their names for you. They should be your friends." She pulled the church program out of her purse and checked it, just in case. "What a nice group the four of you make!" The wind blew the program out of her hands and she waved to it with a shake of her head.

"It wasn't much." She got in the driver's side of the car. "Two minutes, not even that."

"Oh, Lord, I was in heaven."

"I was scared to death." She had almost said "shitless."

TENOR

"It's nothing."

"Let me look at it."

"Don't touch it!"

"Slow down. I can't keep up with you."

"We'll be late."

"I want to help you. I'm scared to death for you."

BASS

Many carols dealt with roses, variants on "Lo, How a Rose," several with the title "A Spotless Rose," as if to emphasize that aspect of the story. He remembered a particular version from college, set to music by the great English composer Herbert Howells. He remembered it because of the baritone solo in the middle, which he had sung. There was no record of the fact.

He wanted to sing it again, forty years later, but in certain measures the choral accompaniment was broken into eight parts. SSAATTBB. Donna's choir could never perform such a piece. She was nervous enough about four-part music and had insisted, "No polyphony." No chanting, either, but then again this was a Methodist church—grape juice for Communion, chunks of white bread, lots of camp meeting hymns, and, for some reason, on page 130, Howells's great hymn tune "Michael," which they had never sung at his old church. He asked Donna to put it in the program sometime, when the occasion was right.

"When would the occasion be right?"

"Howells wrote it after his son died. Michael."

In Howells's "Spotless Rose," the choir had sung like a string accompaniment for the baritone soloist, stretching long vowels across several measures until one forgot they were human voices and believed that the choir had become a chamber orchestra. That's what he had been thinking, long ago, as he sang his solo, carried along by the beautiful accompaniment.

He owned a tape of King's College Choir singing the Howells carol (with two others—"Here Is the Little Door" and "Sing Lullaby"), and perhaps that was what he remembered, a more perfect version overlaying the imperfection of what he had really done, the wrong notes, bad vowels, and shortness of breath.

SOPRANO

She immediately stretched out on Elizabeth's couch and closed her eyes. "Okay, the first question of the day is, what did you think of it?"

"Think of what?"

"My performance!"

"I had my own solo, darling. At exactly the same time. I'm sorry."

"Mine wasn't a solo. It was a quartet."

"Well, then, no big deal."

"It was perfect." She rolled her head on the pillow. Her hair felt dry and brittle, her scalp itched. Vitamins. Folic acid. She wasn't getting enough. "That's what the people said."

"Did they pay you?"

"Donna might start paying me after New Year's. No written contract. But the money doesn't matter."

"I got a hundred dollars for my solo."

"Wow."

"Let me tell you, darling, a hundred dollars wasn't nearly enough for what I went through." Elizabeth collapsed into a beanbag chair.

"What?"

"A deaf organist, a loud cougher in the audience, a feral baby, bad incense—but we're not talking about me, darling. This is your time. Tell me how it went. It was 'perfect.' What does that mean? Isn't that a rather bold statement to make about a musical performance?"

"Don't you believe me?"

"Yes, I believe you." Elizabeth came over and knelt next to the couch. She began petting her hands. "I don't know what I was thinking. Music can be perfect. It's all a question of point of view, of how you define that word. Yes, I really believe that your performance was perfect, darling."

ALTO

They were flying over a desolate part of the country, an abstract pattern of alternating gray and white. Perfect. The hum of the airplane blocked out everything. Not just the screaming babies, but the lingering chords of the beautiful carol. The airplane hummed in F major, and she wanted to be in E, where she had been three days ago, suspended in time.

TENOR

She told him not to get on the plane, gripped his arm. Pleaded with him not to leave so soon.
"Why not, Kathy?"
"You're sick. You shouldn't be traveling."
"I have to get back to work."
"Take a vacation."
"No."

BASS

Donna began baking for him. Crescent rolls, heavy German cakes, her special cinnamon bread, with threads of white icing across the top. At home after rehearsal he ate one slice of it and vomited.

He didn't tell her this, so she kept bringing baked goods to rehearsal, not to share with the whole choir, but for him, hidden in a brown paper bag. The latest was a pan of sweet rolls in the shape of a heart.

"Take it easy, lady."
"You're awfully thin," she said. "My next project is to fatten you up."
"I'm fine."
"No sir, in the last couple of months you've lost weight."
"Don't worry about me, Donna. Have I ever missed a rehearsal? Have I ever missed church service?"
"No. You're very loyal to the choir. You know the music better than

anybody. You could skip rehearsal and still do fine. But please don't skip rehearsal." She pinched him on the side. "Not even a tenth of an inch. You're all skin and bones, and not even that."

"Isn't it enough that I'm holding the bass section together for you?"

"Just barely holding it together. You could use a little *oomph* on those low notes."

"Sorry."

She pinched him again. "If you gained twenty pounds, I think you'd get those low notes back."

"I don't think I ever had them."

SOPRANO

"I really believed things would be different in that church, you know?" She opened her eyes. She had lost track of time. A spider was crawling across Elizabeth's ceiling. The place was filthy, every square inch of it. "I really believed I had found a home for myself."

"You have a lovely home, darling. From what I hear."

"Come on, Elizabeth. You're interrupting me with the same old nonsense. You know what I'm talking about."

"A home? Oh, you mean a church home."

"I wanted to be comfortable there. It wouldn't bother me if I sang in a choir where they had a dozen sopranos and they were all better singers than me. At least I could sing comfortably." She closed her eyes and breathed through her nose.

"Really?"

"Yes, really."

"Your husband takes such good care of you. He keeps you looking young."

"Hah!"

"I could use a husband like that. You know, unlike certain people in this room, I actually have to sing for my supper, I'm that close to the edge."

"I wish you wouldn't interrupt with your own problems, Elizabeth. In ten minutes you'll be sending me out the door and in fifteen minutes you'll be telling Mona how great she is."

"You're my best singer. I'm only trying to offer some perspective."

"Teach me to sing, dammit."

"There will be no swearing in this studio."

ALTO

It snowed on the island for the first time in several years. The heavy flakes melted when they touched the ground. On her front lawn, the snow stayed for a while, and she made footprints in it, walking a tight circle. She walked the circumference road, early January, around sunset, looking for lights in the windows of the isolated cottages. And music, any kind of music, no matter what risk.

There had been a stone house—limestone, or whitewashed stucco. A fence, about knee-high, comfortable to sit on. Oak trees. A wide lawn, with wrought-iron benches. Four people. Perfect.

TENOR

He couldn't hear the phone when it rang, unless he was sitting next to it. The thing inside his head screamed constantly—often more than one voice, like a satanic duet or trio, on the same vowel, somewhere between ohhh and oooo. He stayed home from work a few days. He went in and read his e-mail. His sister said, "I've been calling you. Are you out all the time?"

BASS

He couldn't hit a low G. Not even first thing in the morning, lying in bed, alone, completely relaxed.

SOPRANO

She had new high notes, way above the staff. She worked them through her head and planned a new repertoire.

ALTO

She hit a high G, while on a walk. Not the G immediately above middle C, but another octave higher. That G, which had never been part of her range, not even when screaming in terror.

She reached out with one hand to catch the note and bring it back, clutch it to her body.

TENOR

At night he heard new music in his head, as if he were now "privileged" to hear messages passed among other species.

BASS

Low C became a major struggle, not the low C that only Larry Hooper could hit, but an octave higher, where some altos could resonate, like Cher. He wasn't a bass anymore. He was afraid to test his upper range, suspecting that his true voice lay up there, an octave above middle C. There were men like that, who sang like women.

He dropped out of the choir without telling Donna.

SOPRANO

"What happened to those other singers?" she asked Donna, as she stood next to her at the table after rehearsal, helping to bag more than a dozen uneaten doughnuts.

"They get sick and die."

"No, they don't. They were young."

"Who?"

"You know, the three people I sang with? On Christmas? They didn't get sick and die." She popped a cinnamon doughnut hole into her mouth. "Did they?"

"Oh, the alto and the tenor were just visiting. I couldn't tell you where they are now. I've forgotten their names."

"What about the bass?"

"Retired."

"He wasn't that old."

Donna turned to look out the window. "No, he wasn't old. But he gave it up." She seemed to be choking. "Gave up singing. I tried my best to keep him in the choir. Another bass might come along. They haven't stopped making them."

"And I thought this was gonna be a great choir to sing in. I swear, they're all tone-deaf."

"Don't worry. Other good singers will come to us. And wasn't it a miracle the four of you were here at the same time together?"

"I don't care about the past! I can't make it through another week of my life just thinking about the goddamn past!"

"You're swearing in church, honey."

ALTO

"Hello."

"Your voice is getting lighter, much nicer."

"That's because I haven't smoked a cigarette in eleven months, Mother dear. And I'm just an overall nicer person."

"Are you singing?"

"No." Not in public, at least. By the time that happened, she'd be a soprano with beautiful long hair.

"Did I ever thank you for helping out with the choir on Christmas? I'm forgetting to do things these days."

"Yes, Mother. Many times." Car headlights passed, a hundred feet away. The cat jumped down from the windowsill. "Every Sunday night, it seems."

"Well, guess what! It turns out somebody made a recording of your quartet! The father of the girl who was originally supposed to sing soprano but she came down with the flu. Kimberly's father. I'll ask him to make me a copy."

"Have you heard the tape?"

"No. But I'll send you a copy, dear. A keepsake of something wonderful. Right?"

"You don't have to."

"But it was so beautiful."

"I'd rather not think about it, Virginia." And now it was snowing again. She could hear the flakes hit the window.

"Are you sad?"

"Not really."

"Well, I am," Virginia said. "At least I speak the truth."

TENOR

Now he worked on remembering the high points, the funny things that had happened in his adult life. He reached back as far as early childhood, to get a fix on each year. What year had it been, for example, when his best friend came down with laryngitis and he had sung a solo while the friend lip-synched? It must have happened in college.

How had he managed to sing without opening his mouth? Had it been any good? Did his friend ever return the favor? The tenor felt this vague sense of having done a lot of favors that had never been returned, favors that could not have been returned. And in his present condition, it was hard to imagine how he could be paid back.

BASS

He watched an Ed Sullivan retrospective, hosted by Bob Newhart. Newhart did a lame imitation of Ed. "He should stick to fake phone conversations. Those were funny." The middle portion featured original-cast Broadway performances, in fuzzy black and white. Julie Andrews. Robert Goulet, in *Camelot,* still in his twenties. Great voice. Julie Andrews singing—it made him cry.

SOPRANO

She would take control of the situation.

She would talk other choir members into signing up for voice lessons. Never too late. Even a woman in her eighties could improve her voice, extend her useful singing life.

She would need three of them to do it—an alto, a tenor, and a bass. To have one good person on each of the other three parts would be enough. Talented people, willing to take voice lessons. If they couldn't afford lessons, she'd help pay for them, set up a scholarship, endowed by "anonymous." Better to keep it a secret, since they might resent her efforts. It would be like a voucher. They could sign up with any teacher in the area.

Except Elizabeth. They'd be better off not studying with Elizabeth, since that woman never dealt with the basic technique of singing, but always assumed technique would emerge automatically when the planets were aligned properly or something.

ALTO

The next summer, on a warm day, with just a light breeze, she walked the road, three miles north from her cottage, toward the mansion where the string quartet had played. The four young people had seemed so out of place, yet so relaxed and well adjusted, so absorbed in their music that they might have played several hours into the evening, into the dark, getting it perfect. She walked around the island three times, twelve or thirteen miles, so far that her feet hurt. Nothing looked the same. The stone house looked abandoned, the lawn was overgrown, her feet ached. And there was no music. Can a person have a dream like that? So detailed. Can you dream about people you've never met?

Virginia sent the tape of the quartet. Except it wasn't the right tape. It was a rough recording of a very confused man evidently working on his memoirs. He seemed to think the world had treated him badly. She listened for ten minutes, then threw it away.

TENOR

He remembered the alto fairly well, but not the soprano. The alto had stood next to him. At one point during the second verse, she had touched him on the shoulder, to turn him a few degrees, so she could hear him better, or see him. He had obliged. He had noticed the color of her eyes, gray, with flecks of gold. Her nose and mouth were beautiful.

BASS

He remembered the soprano, but not the alto. The soprano and bass had formed the top and bottom. He had blended with her, focused on her lips, the way she tipped her head toward him when she sang.

The
Sopranos

I'm talking about something really weird here, something you'll never see unless I sketch it out on the page—the choir, split down the middle, two rows on each side, facing each other, like this:

ALTOS	TENORS	BASSES
TREBLES	TREBLES	TREBLES

TREBLES	TREBLES	TREBLES
ALTOS	TENORS	BASSES

The church straddles the page—the sanctuary to the left, the altar to the right. During Communion, the people would march through the blank space in the middle, between the lines, nodding at us as we sang. Nodding as they counted, keeping track of things. This was a weird choir they were looking at, with plenty to keep track of.

The altos were men, the trebles (sopranos) were boys, and our choir director, Dr. Harrison, was also our organist, seated where you see the word "talking" on the first line of this story.

In the next diagram, I've written in everybody—not their names (I never learned them all), but the parts they sang, using a small font for the trebles, because they were smaller than the rest of us, with smaller voices, in fact, and I had to fit more of them on the line. I'm the tenor on the bottom line, in italics, leaning toward the bass.

ALTO	ALTO	TENOR	TENOR	BASS	BASS	BASS
TREBLE	TREBLE	TREBLE	TREBLE	TREBLE	TREBLE	TREBLE

TREBLE	TREBLE	TREBLE	TREBLE	TREBLE	TREBLE	TREBLE
ALTO	ALTO	TENOR	*TENOR*	BASS	BASS	BASS

If the page were wide enough, I could show you a second set of stalls to the right, between us and the altar, with the same number of seats, enough room for another choir, like a spare if we all got sick at once. When we had probationers (very young trebles not yet allowed to sing), they would sit in those stalls—and behind them, occasionally, a couple of old men nobody ever talked about. They could have been retired singers come back to haunt us, or vagrants from off the streets.

Four tenors. Enough. On Sunday mornings I would have been happier singing bass. My notes stopped cold at E above middle C, and my falsetto was just a yodel. I could sing real tenor only at night. Luckily, on the other side, facing me, two real ones held forth—with a pure, accurate, blended sound that rarely failed. The other tenor on my side, to my left, was a lousy singer. A man in his sixties, he would crack on the high notes, talk too much during service, and get lost, generally.

Think of mirrors, clouded mirrors. One side vaguely mirrors the other. Each of us has a double. The trebles get taller on both sides as you move from right to left. On the right end of the line, they barely sing. They fidget, pick their noses, hit each other, drop their hymnals. On the left end, they're almost men, alert, tense, afraid they'll crack and the choirmaster will send them home for a year.

"Well, what do you think?" the old tenor next to me said.

"Is it okay to talk now?"

"Five minutes. The boss went out for a smoke." He pointed toward the angled wood-framed mirror in which we would have seen the top of our director's head if he'd been seated at the organ. "No smoking in church, you know."

"Sounds fair."

"Harrison used to smoke right here in the church. While he was playing you could see the smoke drifting up from the organ, and when he was mad at us there always seemed to be more of it. But the secondhand smoke—some of the mothers complained. So he steps out for a few minutes, once or twice each rehearsal. Settles his nerves. Besides, we need the break from singing." He twisted his head. "My throat is raw."

"Why don't the boys talk?"

"Different order of discipline. We can talk, they can't." He frisked himself and pulled a box of Luden's from his corduroy jacket, shook the box to make sure it wasn't empty. Just having the cough drops in his pocket was a kind of remedy for a scratchy throat. "The little boys get worked up and then it's impossible to settle them down once Harrison comes back. Wastes time."

On the other side, through the still heads of the opposite trebles, I could see the vague profiles of our counterparts, tenors and basses. Two of the heads were so close, they looked like they were kissing. I didn't say anything.

"Well," my neighbor asked again, "what do you think?"

I hesitated. "It's a pretty good choir. I feel lucky to be singing with you."

"We used to be better," he said. "We've had a few deaths in recent years."

"Rebuilding."

"That's right."

"I'm glad I auditioned."

"You look nervous. Shaking all over." He touched my arm. "Something's making you nervous."

"I'm not nervous." I pulled away from his touch. "It's cold in here."

"You better wear long johns next time," he said.

"Is that what you do?"

He didn't answer. This was a place where conversation died out quickly, as if the music killed it, sucked up the oxygen, demanded more than its quota. One did not need to apologize for failing to complete a sentence; it was assumed that the music had somehow absorbed the thought, consumed it, as a virus might do.

Dr. Harrison's head returned to the mirror, nodded slightly, and we sang. I kept my eyes fixed on the top of that head, for the beat and cues (raised eyebrows), but sometimes my attention slipped to the heads of the singers in the opposite back row. I watched their lips. I couldn't see much, the light being so poor, not much more than a dark oval appearing and disappearing, as in some rudimentary cartoon. One guy raised his hand to his mouth and coughed. Another hand went up and touched something. The music kept going.

At the end of rehearsal, the two sides of the choir exited by different doors.

"See you next week," the old tenor said, wrapping a blue scarf around his neck. "If there is a next week," he added, clearing his throat as he spoke, then swallowing whatever he had cleared from it.

"I don't know your name."

"Maxwell."

"First or last?"

"Doesn't matter. See ya."

"Those guys on the other side," I said. "They kind of vanished. I never saw them up close."

"The two sides never mix," Maxwell said.

"Never?"

"Musically, they might, but socially, almost never."

"Why not?" I zipped up my parka and pulled on my gloves.

"Tradition, I guess."

"You know them, don't you? I mean, you talk to them."

"Not much. It doesn't matter."

"Doesn't matter?"

"It doesn't matter as long as the sound blends out there, in the middle, where the people can hear it, where Harrison puts his microphone to record us for posterity. Everything else, regardless of how strange, doesn't matter. Left-handed, right-handed, Episcopal, Roman Catholic, Jewish, atheist. If they were all Martians on the other side, it wouldn't matter, would it? As long as their voices blended with ours."

"Martians?"

"As long as their voices blended. You seem puzzled. Do I need to draw it for you?"

"No. I can picture it."

MARTIANS	MARTIANS	MARTIANS
	[BLENDED VOICES]	
EARTHLINGS	EARTHLINGS	EARTHLINGS

During the next month, the building warmed up by a few degrees, but I still wore my long johns to church, and my body trembled all the time. It might have been the force of the music, coming from the organ, or from the voices themselves—a sometimes violent mixing together in the space that divided us. My body couldn't shake it off.

Maybe they had repaired the lights, or there was more sun coming in as the days got longer, but I began to make out the faces on the opposite side.

The two altos were high school guys, former trebles who evidently had not graduated to juvenile delinquency. One of them was named Kevin. The other, I don't know. Michael? Kevin had a solo one week, so I caught the name when Dr. Harrison scolded him for coming in a beat late. He really ripped into the poor kid. Kevin looked like he was about to cry, and the kid next to him smiled, as if he might get the important solos from now on.

Skip the tenors for a minute and go to the basses. The one on the far end wore a beard. I say "wore" because his beard looked like something he could take off, a shade too dark for his hair, a little too neat around the edges. Next to him, the middle bass had a very round face, smooth, fat lips, wire-rim glasses, bald head. He shook his head a lot—concerning what, I have no idea. The next bass had long hair in a ponytail. He smiled most of the time, often tilting his head toward the ceiling. I did the same, but could see nothing, just a fuzzy gloom, as if Harrison's old cigarette smoke were still forming a cloud up there.

The two tenors on that side looked very ordinary. Medium everything—hair, height, build, complexion. Age? Late twenties? If they'd switched places I would not have been able to tell. They never faced me directly, as the mirror in which they watched Dr. Harrison's head was mounted on the wall behind us, ten feet toward the sanctuary. So I just got this angle of their faces, a glow or shadow in their cheeks, and I'm sure they never looked at me or thought much about me. Our voices met in the middle, and perhaps blended there, or perhaps slid over each other without meeting at all.

Even at the post-concert wine and cheese party, held at Dr. Harrison's apartment across the street from the church, men only, minimum age sixteen—even then, no introductions were offered, and I could not tell who was who. I finally learned a couple of names on my side. The bass next to me, it turned out, lived just one street over from my place. Name was Dick, he told me, though others called him Rick. He had a son on the opposite side middle, a small treble named Eric or Evan or Aaron.

We browsed through Harrison's apartment, examining the artifacts. Pictures of former choirs, here and on tour. Framed awards and ribbons and proclamations. Dick explained things to me, in vague, suggestive ways.

We stopped at a silver-framed eight-by-ten color photograph. Two beautiful women in evening gowns and tiaras stood on some outdoor stage, pointing at each other with fans.

"What's this?" I asked.

"That's right, you're new this year," Dick said, suppressing a laugh. "You've never been to one of those."

"One of those?"

"Too hard to explain," he said. "Ask Maxwell. If you're lucky, he might break down and invite you to this year's extravaganza."

"Invite me?"

"You're looking at his place in the picture. He's very rich, you know." Dick gave me a puzzled look. "You don't know?"

"I know next to nothing. And who are the women?" I asked.

He looked at me again. "You really don't know, do you?"

But I got invited, by telling Maxwell I spent my weekends watching television. Springfield was really dead, compared to my previous city. Maxwell hesitated before inviting me. He kept looking at me from every angle, as if I were up for sale, or in need of some medical diagnosis. He finally said, "I hope you won't be disappointed. It doesn't amount to much. They shouldn't call it an extravaganza."

I drove out to Maxwell's place by myself. Dick was supposed to carpool with me, but when I called him that morning he said, "No, sorry. Once is enough. I got better things to do at home. You can tell me all about it tomorrow." This was a Saturday in late May, our season almost over. I doubted I would come back in the fall. I'd just been laid off again, and thirty dollars a week from singing in choir would not cover the rent.

They billed it as a benefit for the choir—a fundraiser to pay our salaries. I parked along the highway, then walked past a line of cars that filled the long driveway. The house was set on a knoll overlooking the river—one of those octagonal brick deals from the mid–nineteenth century, with white trim and a fancy tower on top. Rich. Maxwell lived there by himself, I think. He'd inherited the place from his parents.

A servant—some tall, long-haired guy in an apron—asked me for my twenty bucks, then looked at me funny and said, "Oh, that's right, you're one of the choir. Free admission for you." He escorted me through to the back of the house. I didn't really get a good look at the inside of the house, except to notice a lot of art on the walls, and I thought, Maybe he is rich. I stepped out the back door into the audience, and Maxwell waved at me and pointed to an empty chair, so I sat there. They were all waiting for something. A plywood stage had been set up in front of us, with an upright piano and bench, and two cabana-type tents off to each side. Dr. Harrison came out of one tent and stepped up onto the stage, kind of heaving himself with an awkward limp. He had a cigarette in one hand, which he set in an ashtray on top of the piano. He was dressed casually, in khaki pants and a light blue Banlon shirt. He nodded to the audience of almost a hundred, then sat down on the bench.

Like this:

| CABANA | PIANO | CABANA |

Tilt the piano forty-five degrees, so that the *O* drops toward the bottom line, then put Dr. Harrison where the *N* was.

I looked at the men around me. I recognized Maxwell, of course, and the bald guy and bearded guy from the opposite side, and one of the basses from our side, and one alto, who seemed a bit young for this crowd. The rest of the men were, like, "friends of music," I figured. They acted like they knew me, but I'd never seen them before.

I had soloed in one of the concerts that winter, actually stepped out from the stalls and stood where the congregation could see my face. That must have been how they knew me.

Dr. Harrison played a light, bouncy prelude. He was a better piano player than organist, his timing more exact, the notes flowing more smoothly. He took a couple of drags off his cigarette, coughed lightly, as if giving a cue.

Then the tent flaps flew open and two women walked out, climbed the steps and stood on opposite ends of the stage. I expected a little dance, but they didn't move. They wore long gowns, matching gloves, and their hair hung loose to their bare shoulders, kind of silver blond. To tell the truth, they looked like twins, identical except for the color of the gowns: red on the left, green on the right.

"Like Christmas," a stranger near me said.

"We could throw tinsel at them," another said, not with any levity, really, just in a flat, ordinary voice.

"Did you bring tinsel?"

"Of course. I always bring tinsel."

Someone laughed, high-pitched, girlish. The two women kept their cool, smiled slightly.

The piano started up again, and the red one sang for a while. In German, I think. Not English. Very high soprano, with a touch more vibrato than I like, but on pitch, and nicely rounded. Eighteenth century. She turned only slightly from side to side as she sang, moved her head just enough to show she wasn't a statue. It puzzled me why the other woman had come up on stage at the same time, as she had nothing to do with this piece. She just stood there and waited, her gloved hands clasped in front, head slightly bowed. Actually, I looked at her rather than at the one who was singing. The piece kept going. Nice, but not exciting. Nobody threw tinsel, and I doubted that they had brought any.

During a break between songs, I turned to the stranger on my right, a guy in sunglasses and a blond crewcut. I asked, "Is there a program for this?"

"Who needs a program?" he whispered.

"I do."

"Really?"

"I came in late. I must have missed something."

"Just watch and listen. You don't need a program," he said. "That would spoil everything."

"Names?"

"Oh," he said, looking at me, nodding slowly, "you wouldn't want to know their names."

"Why not?"

"If you have to ask, then you don't need to know."

"I sing in the choir."

"I knew that," he said.

When it came her turn to sing, the woman in the green dress moved next to the piano. She bent toward Dr. Harrison and said a few soft words to him, and then he nodded, shuffled his music, and began to play. I liked this piece better, with its folk melody, vaguely Irish. I expected this twin to sing alto, offering some contrast with the first performer, but she turned out to be another soprano. Not exactly the same, not her vocal twin—very pure, in the St. Olaf style; that is, with so little vibrato that one feared that the singer might fall off pitch. But she didn't. And she moved when she sang, rolling her head slightly, even lifting her gloved hand to touch her chin from time to time. She sang in English. Simple, longing. I forget the text. I remember the tune, though. She performed two other songs. Her fellow soprano remained on stage all the while, not moving, very much the statue. At the end, they both took bows, then embraced each other— the way musical people do. The audience applauded enthusiastically, whistling and shouting. Still no tinsel.

Maxwell announced an intermission, with refreshments. The sopranos descended from the stage and walked back into their tents, where, I assume, they sat or stood, replaying in their heads how well they had sung. Maybe they stretched out on cots, too exhausted to think about anything. I never saw them again. I needed a program. I mixed with the crowd, but they kind of shunned me. I looked at the tents, but nobody came out of them. The intermission kept going— ten minutes, fifteen, twenty. Food and drink. Maybe that was it. The extravaganza.

I slipped away after a while, drove home. I kept hearing the folk tune that the second soprano had sung, a simple tune, five notes all in the same octave. In my head, it rang in the treble clef, but when I tried to sing along, my voice cracked.

The next morning I went to church, well rested, in excellent voice, the first to arrive.

"Good thing you can sing," Maxwell said, hanging up his cardigan sweater.

"You're not feeling okay?"

"Oh, I'm fine," he said. "But we need you on the tenor this morning. I'm relieved you showed up."

"I always do."

"Thought maybe you were sick," he said.

"I'm not sick."

"You left early, yesterday."

"I did?"

"Never mind, I'm just glad you made it this morning."

"Did I miss something?"

"Can't talk now," he said and covered his mouth with his hand.

We warmed up on a hymn, singing parts on all verses. We sounded awful—no blend at all. Dr. Harrison went out for a smoke. I squinted across the aisle toward our counterparts, thinking some of the men might be missing. All the heads were in place. The church seemed darker than ever, and the heads in the back row opposite had become nothing but silhouettes. They hardly moved. I thought, maybe that's all they are: cutout silhouettes, the kind they use in movies so they don't have to pay extras in crowd scenes. Like this:

XXXXXXX	XXXXXXX	XXXXXXX
TREBLES	TREBLES	TREBLES

"I have to rearrange the music," Dr. Harrison announced when he came back from his smoke. His voice seemed especially low and gravelly. "We'll sing everything in unison this morning, and we'll just do a simple mass right out of the hymnal. Any complaints?"

No complaints. This choir never objected when things were made easier for them. We took our usual half-hour break before church service. I went up to Maxwell and asked, "What happened?"

"The other two tenors are incapacitated this morning. They're here, but they've lost their voices."

"I don't see them. Where'd they go?"

"They're here," he repeated.

"You and I could have carried the part."

"Harrison doesn't think so."

"He told you that?"

"No, but he only lets me sing in this choir because I'm rich. I sing for free, you know. If he had to pay me to sing, I'm sure he wouldn't." His voice trailed off. "I'm not very good."

"Well," I said, failing to contradict him as he must have expected me to do, "I could have gone over to the other side and helped."

"That's a difficult adjustment."

"How?"

"Let me see if I can make it simple for you." He held out both hands in front of him, weighing things in them. "It's as if you had always looked out your right eye, and then suddenly switched to your left eye. Or you were used to driving on the right side of the road and then you had to drive on the left. Know what I mean? Like when you've been driving in France for a couple weeks and you ferry your car over to England and have to make that adjustment?"

"I can picture it," I said.

ROAD IN ENGLAND

"Through the Looking Glass"

ROAD IN FRANCE

"It's an impossible adjustment," he said.

"I'll go over there right now," I said.

"Those guys wouldn't let you. They would never make a place for you over there."

"What am I? An alien?"

He waited too long before answering, "Not at all."

"They don't even know me."

"It's nothing personal."

"If they can't sing, they should have stayed home."

He smiled, patted his back pocket. "In this choir, you have to show up to get paid, and they probably need the money."

"Is it something infectious?"

"No," he said. "It's not infectious. Nothing for a guy like you to worry about."

"They just can't sing, right?"

"Right." He dropped a Luden's into his mouth. "You really don't know, do you?"

"No."

"You had to go home early."

"Yes."

"Well," he said, "I can't tell you anything. And I won't. It's really none of your businesss."

When we sang our first hymn that Sunday morning, the sound felt different. The lower voices seemed thin, overpowered by the upper voices. The soprano part was especially strong, like a high arch that I could walk through without ducking, so high and strong I felt it would never come down.

Last Sunday

Last Sunday we left the church. Our time was up, and we made the best escape we could. A dozen white robes lay in a heap with various anthem books and worship leaflets and cough drop boxes. Two cans of gasoline stood nearby. "Burn, burn, burn," the people chanted, arms waving charismatically. Seated at the organ was a fat effigy in a white robe, drooping head in a black ski mask, rubber knife in its back. Message clear—the choir had to go.

There was a hole in the roof. A helicopter dropped a cable and lifted us through that hole, one by one in a wicker basket—to wild applause, cheering, foot-stomping. They were happy to get rid of us and our fancy anthems, our impossible leader. Yes, they clapped and stomped while a quartet of guitar strummers and tambourine bangers went at it—some Christian rock group. Our replacements.

I was the last to be evacuated—the bravest, the youngest, and the healthiest. The most reluctant. I rather enjoyed the guitars, could have adapted. Instead, here I was in this wicker basket, bumping against the rafters as the chopper hauled me out of the building, and you would have thought at least *one person* in that goddamn church would regret my departure, would reach up and claw at the basket and call out my name, as if I were some rock legend—"Jerry, we need you! We love you!" No. They hated me. A round of gunfire went off as the basket swung clear of the roof. I could never go back. It was a country that I had left for good.

As we rose above the city, the helicopter shuddered violently. I dug my fingers into my knees. Carol lit up a cigarette, offered me one.

"No thanks." I still cared about my throat and lungs, still thought there were places in the world that might ask me to sing. "What about Paul?" I asked. "What's he gonna do now—direct a choir in another town?"

Carol shook her head. "Nobody will hire him. They know."

"Like, the *whole country* knows?"

"Yes," she said. "They know what he supposedly did, and he can't get work anywhere."

"Is there a law that alerts unsuspecting churches as to the identity of abrasive choir directors?"

"Yes."

"Posters of their guilty faces, faxed across the country, nailed to telephone poles?"

"Yes."

The helicopter climbed and the city grew small below us. In one glance I could make out the steeples of a dozen other churches. None would take us. *They knew.* We crossed the river and headed north, banking slightly as we followed the main highway through the suburbs. That would be my house directly below—in flames, the roof collapsing. And then, perhaps a mile farther north, Paul's house, reduced to a smoking ruin. An important bridge was out. Flashing lights, traffic being rerouted onto secondary roads.

Nobody felt like singing. We looked at each other, lips sealed, hands hidden in pockets. Eight of us. There had been ten or twelve when we marched to the choir stalls that morning, white robes over combat fatigues. A couple of the older ones must have defected during evacuation, thinking, "If I leave, what church will bury me?" They had stayed behind, covering their ears as they hid among the empty pews in the front of the church.

I bowed my head, but not in prayer. The chopper blades cut through all my reasons for feeling unappreciated. They destroyed the music, measure by measure and note by note, vibrating and bending harmony into dissonance and, finally, into silence. Thus had the music disintegrated, its meaning now broken into tiny crumbs that lodged in the folds of my voicebox and kept me from singing, kept me from even remembering what good singing had been like. *Where was middle C? What was the difference between a quarter note and a half note? Between an alto and a tenor? How do you pronounce "God"?* I had no idea.

My feet were cold, my back stiff. My throat was tight and dry. I sucked a honey lemon cough drop, tumbled it between my teeth until it was a delicate sliver balanced on the tip of my tongue, then nothing. The choir sat on benches in two rows facing each other. Most had their heads down, chin to chest, dreaming of what they had lost—for some of them, an entire civilization, decades of loyalty and sacrifice, of pulling sweet music out of the thin and hostile air. Carol chainsmoked, tapping her ashes into a camouflage helmet. The sound of chopper blades settled into a dull whirr. She gave me a sharp nudge. "Get ready, Jerry. We have to jump."

"Have to?"

"It hardly matters to me," she said. "What's there to live for without the choir? I may as well jump and get it over with.",

"Where's Paul?"

"That's a good question."

"Why isn't he with us?"

"If he was," she said with a dry laugh, "then he already jumped." We looked out the window, at the dark valleys where a disgraced choir director might be hiding, might have tumbled in a free fall.

How it began: late winter, frozen and packed into our twelve-foot-square rehearsal space, the basement of the church. Some worker had knocked a hole in the wall large enough to stick your head through, into an unheated and forgotten room full of ancient pews, detached stained glass windows, rusted handbells. I said to Carol, "Probably a couple of dead bodies back there, too," and she gave me a look, as if it was nothing to joke about. We patched the hole the best we could with old church programs, unsingable anthems, get-well cards, whatever was handy. Paul brought in a space heater. But the choir room was always freezing after that, and our singing had a chilled, tentative quality, never rising above mezzo piano. We kept our coats and scarves on through rehearsal, watched our breath rise as we talked or sang. Paul wore gloves and ski cap at the piano, got fat, grew a beard.

He gestured at us with his gloved hands. "It has come to this."

"What are you saying?" Carol asked.

"Nothing works. The organ upstairs is half dead. I'm half dead."

"No you're not," she said. "You have to be strong for us."

"Yeah, I suppose." He played a dissonant chord, then resolved the dissonance. "The best defense is a good offense. How's that? Keep the faith? I swear, the choir is gonna win this thing."

Win this thing? We didn't have a chance. A car backfired and two people screamed.

"That's it," Paul said as he ducked under the piano. "I'm getting a bullet-proof choir robe."

"Get one for everybody."

"Sure. Like they'd put that in the budget."

One rehearsal night the space heater blew out the lights and we sat in the dark room, gripping our hymnals and anthem books, only wanting to *sing*, to defeat chaos in the best way we knew. "It has come to this," our leader said in a rough whisper, which made me touch my neck, massage my throat, pinch and kill whatever bug had entered my body. I found a cough drop in my down vest pocket, deep in there among concert ticket stubs and lint balls. I unwrapped and tasted it. Orange. How long had it been since I gave up orange and switched to honey lemon? Ten years? Orange brought back Mozart and Brahms and four-part polyphony and a high B-flat that I had hit full voice without yelling. A motet by Howells, with a perfect solo, evoked by that singular flavor, which had smoothed out all the rough edges and polished each note like a precious stone. Beneath the orange was a menthol that made my eyes blur.

"What are they doing to us?" a voice asked. "And why?"

"I've begun to keep the phone off the hook," Paul said. "It has come to this. Pray for me."

"We're behind you," Carol said, then coughed. "No matter what."

"I believe you are in *front* of me," Paul said. "Aren't you?"

"Funny," some low voice said.

"Maybe we could laugh at our troubles," another voice said. "That's the best way to deal with them."

"It won't stop the hatred."

The wind sang through the hole in the wall, a tight, three-part harmony.

"Shall we go home?" Paul asked. "Or do you people want to sing?"

"Sing," I said. But the rest said no. They were defeated by the cold and dark, unable to make music without looking at the notes. We set down our books and stumbled out of the choir room. On our way out, Paul said, "You people better hope for good lighting conditions when the shit finally hits the fan. You wanna make a quick escape." This was a slow and reluctant choir, who could not imagine what he meant, whose only response was, "Watch your mouth. We're still in church."

When I drove across the bridge that night, my tires hummed on a low B-flat and I sang against that steady bass line, and later, against the whir of my garage door and the refrigerator and the sleep machine I switched on every night to cover the honking cars—and the phone, before I unhooked it. "Are you for him or against him?" a high-pitched, wormy phone voice had asked. I knew exactly what the question referred to and which of the above I was supposed to be, even if I didn't know who was calling.

I waited a few seconds. "I'm for him."

"I could tell you a story or two."

"Not interested."

"About what he did and who he did it to. You better listen."

"Nope."

"It's gonna get bad then," she said. "For you, too, Jerry."

"I only want to sing beautiful music."

"Bad. Get out now."

My singing voice, outer and inner, connected the random points of any given day, curving around the dark facts that anonymous people wanted to drop in its path. *He hurt Emily. It was terrible. He insulted Judith. She was devastated.* Those kinds of statements. I filled my head with music, so as not to hear them. *Nobody should ever be allowed to talk to a person that way. That's abusive. Because of what he said to her, her voice froze up and she had to go into the psych ward. She spent Christmas there. He's a bad man.*

I had no bone to pick with him. He had never insulted or abused me. It was always, "Jerry, that was perfect." Or, "Jerry, you keep getting better and better." My singing voice. This was what he had done for me—if not materially (I had evidently been born with my talent), then in some intangible sense, as if he had tailored an expensive suit that I could step into without alterations. He had made the very thing that held my life together, the thin wire on which all my random beads were strung. The same assertive finger, which had pointed at Emily or Judith and shattered a tenuous membrane of self-respect, had pointed at me one Sunday morning just a measure before this brilliant solo he had forgotten to assign me in advance—as if to say, "It's your moment of glory, Jerry. You can do it." And I did it. One nod from him, after a perfect solo, was enough to block out all the negative whispering.

There were weeks and weeks and more weeks, into the best pages of the liturgical calendar, when our leader was too sick to get out of bed and Carol would stop by my house to tell me choir rehearsal had been canceled. "This is bad," she would say. "They're taking away the only thing that I live for. And that poor man, this is gonna kill him."

"He's fatally ill?"

"Not quite that."

"Fatally misunderstood."

"That's it." She rolled up her car window, and drove away.

And not long after that, in the middle of Sunday worship, the helicopter came and took us, lifted us out of the church one by one—except the old couple who hid behind the pews, and our leader, who was absent, still "sick," perhaps burned to a crisp in his ruined house, seated at a piano, touching the keys when the firestorm swept through.

The women cried as they stripped off their robes and climbed into the wicker basket. And then the men, tenors and basses, four of us, grim-faced. The wind from the chopper blades pushed old church programs against the back of the sanctuary in a swirl of litter and dead leaves, programs with the names of anthems that would never again be sung in that place, the name of our director, already a forbidden word. Motets and magnificats and medieval chants—I knew all the words and notes, memorized, blended and perfected, my heart and throat brimming with them. I was ready for a last-minute solo. But the helicopter took me, while the electric guitars wailed, the tambourines rang, and the congregation cheered, roaring as if to drive away every good note we had ever sung.

Music of the
Inner Lakes

For a long time I held my left hand in a fist. I held my right hand in a fist, too, as if to protect it from what had happened to the left—that day in the Silver Lake store when my cousin asked, "How thin do you want your turkey?" and I said, "I don't know." A careless gesture, bright blade spinning, the upper joints of my ring and pinkie fingers suddenly disconnected, suspended in air above the slicer, then dropping into a pool of blood.

After five years of self-pity, I opened both fists and gave serious thought to playing guitar again. I reversed the strings and began to retrain my left hand as the picking hand, stood in front of the mirror, made myself dizzy, then tried it again with my eyes closed. No music. That was in July. The guitar sat in its case now, a shadowy figure propped against the wall, pinheaded, bottom-heavy, the only guest in the cottage—and not a happy one. Eventually I would reverse the strings back to their normal sequence and make do with the chords that could be held down with two fingers, get the thumb involved by reaching around to the sixth string. This may sound like the work of a contortionist, but after all, wasn't there an armless woman in Tennessee who played guitar with her toes?

"Such a coward," my cousin said as she bagged my groceries—presliced turkey sealed in plastic, rye bread, beer, pretzels, mayonnaise, canned goods. Last night, scared of rowing across the lake in the rain, I had missed the weekly folk concert at the town museum.

"And how were the fiddlers?"

"Absent. Sick. Food poisoning." Janine frowned at a can of chicken soup, unsure of the price or edibility, and dropped it in my pack without ringing it into the register, kind of waving her hand over the keys as if to appease the god of commerce. "I wish you'd stop being a hermit and hook up your damn phone. When you don't show up on time for something, the first thing I assume is your boat sank." She squinted into a smile, the corner lines of her eyes forming perfect pie-cuts in her ruddy skin.

"It was supposed to rain."

"Went anyway. Hair gets wet, no big deal. I'm about ready to shave it all off, you know." She pulled the concert flyer from the side of the register, balled it up and tossed it in the trash, then clapped her hands, applauding either her good aim or the fact that the concert was over. "Other musicians came up and played, some bad, some good, if you trust my opinion. I took a blanket and sat on the lawn, no mosquitoes. And it didn't rain! At least not on our end of the lake. You would have loved it!" she shouted, almost singing. She slapped her left hand on the counter, kept a steady beat as she described the quartet who had come up on stage as the final act. "You just would have loved those people."

She was talking about the Meekers—locals, very backwoods, occasional store customers. Gas and cigarettes, kerosene in winter. Cash only. No food stamps. Too proud for that. They had a place twenty miles north of Silver Lake, on a desolate road named for the family. Father, mother, brother, sister, no instruments, folk performers of the most primitive kind, sorrowful, repetitive, shocking. They sang everything in octaves and fourths and fifths. "To this beat," Janine said, with a couple more slaps and a forceful stare. She should have recorded it on video. Half the show was how these Meekers looked, their heads stiff and eyes wide open, scared by their own music or by the horrors the music described. "Look how mad you are. Ha! You really missed something!"

I *was* mad, but I was also disgusted with myself, my failure to write any music for the past several years, the frustration of not being able to play. When I got to my boat there was an inch of water in it, a soggy towel, a popsicle wrapper. I set the backpack on the rear seat and grabbed the oars. I looked at my fingers. There might be a song in the horrors of slicing off fingertips, but I would change the story and have it take place on an isolated mountain, twenty miles from help: *My lover was trimming my fingernails. The jackknife slipped.*

Music was seeping back into my life, into the dry soil of neglect, the twisted roots of deprivation and self-pity. I felt this change and finally acted on it. The last concert evening of the summer, 90 percent chance of rain this time, I suddenly felt brave, rowed to the store, poked my head in and asked Janine if she'd go with me. She had overdue bills to pay, waved me out the door with a flyswatter. So I drove six miles to the museum barn alone and sat on a bench and watched the fiddlers perform, a couple of old hippies, one with a long beard, the other ponytailed, as if to keep them straight for us. They were okay, although when they put down their instruments to sing, their voices tended to sag—under pitch, waterlogged, unblended on the back vowels, perhaps the lingering effect of that food poisoning. Folksinging doesn't have to be bad singing, off-pitch. I mean, it's supposed to sound good, and these guys didn't. We were relieved to go back to the lightness of their fiddling, the music lifting them off the floor, it seemed, high above us, this audience of twenty earthbound mortals who had come in out of the rain. I sat alone, cuddling my flask of rum. In my old singing days, I carried a flask inside my jacket and drank from it between numbers, to soothe the calluses on my throat, loosen the strings that rang in my head, a quarter tone sharp.

When the fiddlers had completed their set, the emcee invited audience members to come up and perform. "Hey, don't be shy, I know we got some fine singers out there!" I remained seated—I had not brought my guitar, couldn't play it anyway, and I had no songs. The music had dried out and all the words I had ever written were stranded in that dry streambed of my mind, like broken branches and dead fish.

So the Meekers made their entrance, unannounced, kind of shuffling and bumping into each other. I knew who they were without any introduction. It was warm that night, but they shivered. They hugged themselves and arranged their stiff bodies in a straight line, more than arm's length apart, as if spacing themselves to do calisthenics. Or they might have been asking for new clothes. *Look at us. This is all we own.* The little girl had on pink shorts and a white T-shirt, yard sale rejects. The other three were in jeans and flannel. The mother's hair was wet, flat, hacked. She had a bald spot. The father and son seemed close enough in age to be brothers, shaped the same (left shoulder low, head tipped to the right), wearing identical gray baseball caps, bills forward. They set up a rhythm by slapping their thighs, and the little girl sang a few measures before the men came in with a nasal drone. Jesus this and Jesus that, and *take me now, Lord Jesus.* I had hoped for better. The mother clapped through most of these numbers, sang alto on choruses. They blended well, but the music was too gospel for me, too fiercely hopeful of salvation—which was what must have endeared them to Janine. Finally, the older of the two men cleared his throat and announced, "One more, everybody, then we'll scoot on home. It's called 'Don't Leave Me in the Snow,' and every word is true. Wrong time of year for a song like that, but maybe you'll feel it. If it's any good." He clapped a couple of times, the girl started to sing, then he stopped her with a hand on the shoulder and said to the audience, "You're gonna want the background on this."

The song had something to do with a dark little lake at the end of their property where the road ended and the trail took over, a faint and ghostly footpath that wiggled through thirty miles of true wilderness before it hit the next road. One of the Meekers—evidently there were at least a dozen of them—had hiked to the shore of this lake in early April that year, a few days before the ice went out. At the eastern end of the lake, a half mile away, maybe not even that far, two people came into view, stranded on the ice, waving, shouting for help. They broke through and went down real slow, still calling out as they sank, hands waving for a moment after the heads disappeared. The next day a couple of Meekers ventured out with their shepherd dog and tracked footprints ten miles northeast, up to an abandoned shack at the edge of the snowline. That was where they made a terrible discovery. "Heck, I'm ruining it for you," the father said with a laugh. "We'd better sing the darn thing." So the men slapped their thighs and the little girl sang alone:

Father, father, don't leave me in the snow.
I'm cold and hungry.
Father, father, please don't go.
You seem so angry.

The other voices came in and acted out the parts—the father and the son who came down from the shack and got lost in the fog and scrubby underbrush, finally arriving at the lake and stepping onto the too-thin ice; the mother who stayed behind caring for her daughter until the little girl died, and who then went crazy and wandered into the wilderness, into the endless deep snow. Mrs. Meeker hugged herself as she sang, regretful, almost weeping. The men kept up a good beat on the floor, heavy shoes drumming steady and solid, as the little girl became a ghost and the father and brother sank into the cold lake. From that point, the lower parts evolved into a deep monotonous humming under the child's ghostly wail. The verses kept going, no details excluded. These were the dead, telling their own story, and it was a damn fine song, I thought.

While they sang and beat on the floor, I pressed my thumbnail into the tip of my left index and middle fingers, the ones that were still intact on that hand. They were soft, much too soft. I used to do this in the dentist's chair, as a distraction from the prick of a novocaine needle or the slip of a drill too close to a nerve. Always dealing with pain, of one kind or another. I leaned back and drank from my bottle. The audience clapped along, and the chorus, "Father, father, don't leave me in the snow," became so familiar that I belted out a line or two of it until the little girl gave me the evil eye. I had thrown them off for a measure. But they knew the song well, they had lived it, and I was learning it now, forming chords with missing fingers—E minor, C, D, B minor, phantom chords, invisible lines of concordance where the voices kept crossing and repeating. Luckily it was pretty dark in there, and nobody had to witness such a grotesque performance on my part.

The store lights were off. Janine had closed early and gone to bed. Stars in the sky. No moon. I got into my boat, centered myself, laid the flashlight on the rear seat, pointing over the stern to illuminate the perfect wake. My fingers formed chords as I rowed, mostly E minor and D major, and I kept beat with the oar strokes, hardly noticing when the rain began to fall again, hardly feeling the chill. Far to the east, moving toward the point, two sets of headlights stitched a hem along the dark skirt of the lake, defining its vast shapelessness.

They had found the girl's body in the shack, on a stained mattress, hard and cold. She held a hairless rag doll, with a grip so tight they had to bury her that way. She wore a dirty pink sweatshirt, polyester slacks. Her feet were bare. The old stove was slightly less cold than every other surface. Someone had burned pages from a Bible. Ice had formed in a low corner, and caught in that ice was a dead mouse, lying on its back.

I had already hiked most of the trails in the county and marked them brown on my 1945 map, over the faint broken lines that often represented trails that had faded away in the years since the map was drawn, ghost trails. Meeker Road lay beyond my usual range. It was my rule never to drive more than twice as far as I intended to hike—drive ten miles to the trailhead, then walk at least five miles in; drive twenty miles, then walk at least ten, but ten was pushing my physical limit for day hikes, and I never carried a sleeping bag or stove, never slept in the woods. Too much of a coward, I told Janine. My cousin hadn't gone up there in many years. She wanted to do this. In the dead time between Labor Day and peak color, she had turned off the gasoline pumps and closed the store for an afternoon. "You're not a coward," she told me. "This is much more of an adventure than going to a little concert at the barn."

I needed to do this. I needed to get in there, way in there, to the place where the songs had come from, deep into a wilderness that I had only touched the surface of.

We drove parallel to the winding river, past the old ski area and over the divide into balsam country, with only an occasional flare of maple red to remind us of the season. I was making up stuff, telling her that the people in the ice-breaking song were distant cousins of the Meekers, holed up in the mountains for the winter, living on venison, drinking melted snow, burning their Bible to keep warm. She said, "That's nothing. I'm probably related to those people. We had a renegade cousin up here in the woods, long time ago."

"So it's in the blood!" In my best voice I sang the chorus for her. "Father, father, don't—"

"My blood. Not yours. And mine is very much thinned out, I'm sure."

I tapped the steering wheel with my mangled fingers, where she could see them. "You don't like my singing."

"It's just that one person can't do four-part harmony, and I'm not good enough to imagine it on my own."

After a moment I said, "Not enough of us around to make a group, right?" I looked at her. "Our family?"

"Don't include me. I can't carry a tune."

Meeker Road was paved the first hundred yards, after which rough asphalt turned to ribbed dirt. The power line shunted into the ground. Yellow signs marked the curves or warned of a narrow bridge, a hairpin turn, children at play. We passed a trailer that was nearly consumed by its scaly wooden additions, then a *Deaf Child Area* sign, faded almost to white, bullet-ridden, and perhaps no longer necessary. There might be a song in how that had happened. *Father, father, please don't shoot, I couldn't hear you.* The road cut into the steep side of a mountain, its surface tipped out so as to drain quickly, curving down into a flat area of dead trees, a brief widening, and a sign for a bus stop.

"Who's the deaf child?" I asked.

"Buddy Meeker. He's almost thirty now, finally graduated high school. At least they gave him a diploma."

"Not one of the singing Meekers."

Janine shook her head.

"Not even, like, the B-team."

"No."

The road narrowed to one lane under a canopy of beech and ancient white pine, grass down the median, loose gravel, not much more than a jeep trail. There was a tarpaper cabin on the right, an old bus on the left, a sagging gray house straight ahead. It was the end of the road, with no space to turn the car around. There had to be dogs out here, mad dogs bred with coyotes, chained up or held back by an unreliable hand. No sign that this was the Meeker place, like a mail-box with musical notes painted on it. Nothing like that.

"They're not home," Janine said.

"They're touring. They've gone to Nashville."

"Right. If they block our car, we'll be forced to talk to them." She rolled up her window. "They might let their dogs out, or something worse."

"Let's hike. We'll meet them in the woods."

"You're not such a coward," she said again, stepping out carefully.

Well, I had my fears. But the air smelled so nice and sweet and my mind was clearing. I was ready for just about anything.

We locked the car and began hiking a dry path into the state wilderness, staying close enough to talk. Janine knew the territory—the ghost towns, the tanneries and sawmills that had thrived a hundred years ago, the small upland lakes formerly connected by road to the outer world. A single overgrown trail now threaded that mysterious fabric. This was old farmland, never productive of anything except misery, too rocky, too steep, too cold. Janine pointed to the remnants of stone walls, property lines. Ice caves. Coldest temperatures in the state. An ancestor from the last century, another poor cousin who lived in this valley, had gone out to chop wood one morning. He froze solid, standing up, ax in midswing.

"That's folklore," I laughed.

"It's a good story," Janine said. "Write a song about it. If you don't want it I'll give it to the Meekers next time they come to the store." She shivered, although the temperature was at least sixty.

I didn't see any lake where the Meekers' song claimed it would be. A swamp, no more than that. The path followed a stream, an outlet from a chain of lakes that lay ten miles east of us. Janine called them the "inner lakes," her voice sucking in on the s, as if the water of the lakes needed to be contained that way. The property had been owned by her father's family until the twenties, sold to International Paper, then to the state, all structures removed at that time. More were built later, illegally—hunting shacks, tent platforms, lean-tos cobbled out of wrecked snowmobiles and broken skis—by loners who shopped for food once or twice a year. Janine did business with such men, assumed they had families from what they bought: the toys, women's magazines, crossword puzzle books, children's aspirin, a case or two of infant formula. They paid cash, these men from the inner lakes. They never spoke, hardly breathed through their thick red beards.

"Lost River," she said, her voice sucking in again.

"Good name for another song."

"Oh, don't bother. They already wrote it. The Meekers did. Everything they wrote came out of this godforsaken place." In fact, they had sung it the evening I stayed home, afraid of the rain and the dark. "Lost River," Janine repeated. She picked up a dead branch and flung it toward the stream, waited for the splash. "The name of the song. It was great. 'Lost River, Lost River,' " she chanted, " 'Hid away, where grandpa lay, darkest day, darkest day . . .' "

Damn those Meekers. I wanted a virgin trail to take me into this part of my life, or, if not virgin, at least not so heavily trampled in recent years. I didn't want to keep hearing that some other party had arrived ahead of me, grabbed all the good songs, and sung them in public. Janine lagged behind as the path got steeper. In her pale flat voice, she sang for a while, alone, and then with other voices. Or it may have been the wind accompanying her, blowing across the hard edges of a well-tuned forest.

Whenever I hiked, I carried a stick, dead wood, a device to measure the measureless, snapping off inch-long segments at odd intervals. There was a music in that, too, a music in walking, in the shifting and dimming light that came down through the trees, now mostly yellow birch and hemlock. There was music in crossing the contours of this upland, as I had seen them drawn on a map, tight and parallel like a musical staff, five lines for every hundred feet of elevation. The whole landscape was fretted as we climbed higher, and not just the sound of water falling across the straight lines of more resistant rock, but also the tree roots that held back the soil in even steps, and the going back in time, across years and decades, time held back by the regrowth of the forest and the narrowing of the trail.

It's too late, I said to myself. I meant late in the day, but it was late in the year, late in the decade. My dead stick was entirely gone, all the pieces scattered, and if I wasn't careful I'd soon be breaking off finger-tips. We had to turn around, even though, by now, we had begun to follow footprints, frozen hard in this dry mud, toes pointed down-hill—toward us.

And I would have turned around if I hadn't seen a set of prints in fresh mud, toes pointed the other direction—into the wilderness. They were sneaker prints, child-size, not much bigger than my hand, and so clear that they looked as if they had been deliberately placed there as false evidence. The muddy area tapered into dry leaves and the sneaker prints faded as the trail shot up over a piney ridge and then back down toward the creek, which was roaring now with the water that had spilled down from the inner lakes. We were two miles in, maybe more. I thought of how she had said it, the *s* at the end of *lakes,* drawn out like static that covered the truth, a string of words she would not articulate, the truth, always withheld from me. I stopped for a minute, called out "Janine!" and then moved ahead slowly, waiting for her reply. The creek was too loud. I grabbed another walking stick.

When the roar of the creek subsided, a drumming sound took over, or an axe slowly chopping. I called out for Janine again. The drum-ming seemed too dull to be an axe, too musical. It might have been some animal language, a huge bird warning me off, or a couple of sheep knocking their heads together—remnant of a domestic flock, now wild and big-horned.

A sharp turn in the trail revealed a skinny boy in a torn gray shirt and black jeans, whacking a big stick against a hollow tree trunk.

I coughed, then called out, but he didn't hear me. I shouted, "Whatcha doing?" and he still didn't turn to answer. I tapped his shoul-der with my walking stick and he swung around, flailing his stick like a sword.

"Are you Buddy Meeker?" I asked.

He held the stick in front of his chest, mouth open, and grunted in a low voice, no recognizable words or tune. This was one weird-looking kid, with his continuous eyebrow, dirty blond caveman hair, ears sticking out much too high on his head, like a cat's. His shirt was ragged, jeans threadbare. He might have been twelve, fourteen, eighteen, twenty-eight. He might have been a Meeker, or something more primitive—of which the Meekers were a cleaned-up version, sent out into the world to perform. This was it. This was the kind of thing they had been singing about. Except for a slight tremor in my amputated fingertips, I did not move, afraid the kid would hit me with his stick.

He said nothing. He was painfully skinny, concave. There were welts on his face and neck.

"I'm sorry," I finally said, and the boy seemed to relax, dropped his stick, scratched his funny ears. I set down my stick and held out my empty hands, a gesture of peace. He smiled and reached into the hollow tree, from which he pulled a handful of swarming beetles or termites, held them out for my inspection, and after a couple of seconds, shoved them in his mouth. The bugs seemed to vibrate inside his neck for a second before he swallowed them, buzzing for that brief moment, more articulate than any sound he could make. That's what I thought about, not the grossness of it. He pounded his chest—hollow, like the tree, but in a higher octave, reached into the tree trunk again and pulled out another handful, offering them to me. I stepped back and shook my head. He ate the bugs, then grabbed his stick and took off, northeast, deeper into the wilderness, his feet hardly touching the ground.

This was it. And, no doubt, there was more of it, higher up, hidden—conjoined twins, people with dog heads, chicken heads, a world of wonder that had never been set to music. Yes, I would have followed the boy to it, if not for Janine.

"Are you lost—are you lost—are you lost—are you lost?" Janine's anxious voice echoed through the valley, as I stood by the hollow tree, drumming a beat with my walking stick. Bang, bang, pause. Bang, bang, pause. I was deep in the wilderness now, deep and rooted in the place where the songs began, the place where I would begin to write again. I kept beating, as if to coax a melody out of the tree trunk. The dead wood had a definite tone that rang back through my arms and into my whole body. Low E-flat. Very low. An owl hooted somewhere nearby, mad at me, or oblivious to my presence. B-flat. Another bird sounded as if it was crying—two notes, C and F, the second note drooping in extreme sorrow. "Are you lost—are you lost—are you lost?" Already, I was making a song of those words, setting them to the rhythms and notes that I had picked up. The sad thing about the song was that, in many ways, I was still standing on the surface of this world. I had not broken through.

I lay down in pine needles and rolled to one side. Some of the needles poked into my left ear and strummed three chords along the very top of my hearing. The upper branches of a dead beech, shaped like a disfigured hand, raked across the deep blue sky, and I heard that, too.

Roger Sheffer teaches creative writing at Minnesota State University, Mankato. His previous collections of short fiction are *Lost River* (Night Tree Press, 1988) and *Borrowed Voices* (New Rivers Press, 1990). His fiction has appeared in such magazines as *Adirondack Life, Another Chicago Magazine, BlueLine, The Missouri Review,* and *Laurel Review.* When not teaching and writing, he sings in Musicorum, a chamber choir based in Mankato. Sheffer recently released a CD of folk music, *The Boy in the Window,* produced in collaboration with guitarist Jim McGuire.